William Morris, Alfred J. Wyatt

Tale of Beowulf

Sometime King of the Folk of the Weder Geats

William Morris, Alfred J. Wyatt

Tale of Beowulf
Sometime King of the Folk of the Weder Geats

ISBN/EAN:

Printed in Europe, USA, Canada, Australia, Japan

Cover: Foto ©Andreas Hilbeck / pixelio.de

More available books at **www.hansebooks.com**

THE TALE OF BEOWULF

BIBLIOGRAPHICAL NOTE

*First printed at the Kelmscott Press, January
1895
New Edition, August 1898*

THE TALE OF BEOWULF SOMETIME KING OF THE FOLK OF THE WEDER GEATS TRANSLATED BY WILLIAM MORRIS AND A. J. WYATT

LONGMANS, GREEN, AND CO.
39 PATERNOSTER ROW, LONDON
NEW YORK AND BOMBAY
MDCCCXCVIII

Printed by BALLANTYNE, HANSON & Co.
At the Ballantyne Press

ARGUMENT

HROTHGAR, king of the Danes, lives happily and peacefully, and bethinks him to build a glorious hall called Hart. But a little after, one Grendel, of the kindred of the evil wights that are come of Cain, hears the merry noise of Hart and cannot abide it; so he enters thereinto by night, and slays and carries off and devours thirty of Hrothgar's thanes. Thereby he makes Hart waste for twelve years, and the tidings of this mishap are borne wide about lands. Then comes to the helping of Hrothgar Beowulf, the son of Ecgtheow, a thane of King Hygelac of the Geats, with fourteen fellows. They are met on the shore by the land-warder, and by him shown to Hart and the stead of Hrothgar, who receives them gladly, and to whom Beowulf tells his errand, that he will help him against Grendel. They feast in the hall, and one Unferth, son of Ecglaf, taunts Beowulf through jealousy that he was outdone

by Breca in swimming. Beowulf tells the true
tale thereof. And a little after, at nightfall,
Hrothgar and his folk leave the hall Hart, and
it is given in charge to Beowulf, who with his
Geats abides there the coming of Grendel.

Soon comes Grendel to the hall, and slays a
man of the Geats, hight Handshoe, and then
grapples with Beowulf, who will use no weapon
against him : Grendel feels himself over-mastered
and makes for the door, and gets out, but leaves
his hand and arm behind him with Beowulf : men
on the wall hear the great noise of this battle
and the wailing of Grendel. In the morning
the Danes rejoice, and follow the bloody slot of
Grendel, and return to Hart racing and telling
old tales, as of Sigemund and the Worm. Then
come the king and his thanes to look on the
token of victory, Grendel's hand and arm, which
Beowulf has let fasten to the hall-gable.

The king praises Beowulf and rewards him,
and they feast in Hart, and the tale of Finn and
Hengest is told. Then Hrothgar leaves Hart,
and so does Beowulf also with his Geats, but the
Danes keep guard there.

In the night comes in Grendel's Mother, and
catches up Aeschere, a thane of Hrothgar, and
carries him off to her lair. In the morning is

Beowulf fetched to Hrothgar, who tells him of this new grief and craves his help.

Then they follow up the slot and come to a great water-side, and find thereby Aeschere's head, and the place is known for the lair of those two : monsters are playing in the deep, and Beowulf shoots one of them to death. Then Beowulf dights him and leaps into the water, and is a day's while reaching the bottom. There he is straightway caught hold of by Grendel's Mother, who bears him into her hall. When he gets free he falls on her, but the edge of the sword Hrunting (lent to him by Unferth) fails him, and she casts him to the ground and draws her sax to slay him ; but he rises up, and sees an old sword of the giants hanging on the wall ; he takes it and smites off her head therewith. He sees Grendel lying dead, and his head also he strikes off ; but the blade of the sword is molten in his venomous blood. Then Beowulf strikes upward, taking with him the head of Grendel and the hilts of the sword. When he comes to the shore he finds his Geats there alone ; for the Danes fled when they saw the blood floating in the water.

They go up to Hrothgar's stead, and four men must needs bear the head. They come to Hrothgar, and Beowulf gives him the hilts and tells him what he has done. Much praise is given to Beowulf; and they feast together.

On the morrow Beowulf bids farewell to Hrothgar, more gifts are given, and messages are sent to Hygelac: Beowulf departs with the full love of Hrothgar. The Geats come to their ship and reward the ship-warder, and put off and sail to their own land. Beowulf comes to Hygelac's house. Hygelac is told of, and his wife Hygd, and her good conditions, against whom is set as a warning the evil Queen Thrytho.

Beowulf tells all the tale of his doings in full to Hygelac, and gives him his gifts, and the precious-gemmed collar to Hygd. Here is told of Beowulf, and how he was contemned in his youth, and is now grown so renowned.

Time wears; Hygelac is slain in battle; Heardred, his son, reigns in his stead, he is slain by the Swedes, and Beowulf is made king. When he is grown old, and has been king for fifty years, come new tidings. A great dragon finds on the sea-shore a mound wherein is stored the treasure of ancient folk departed. The said dragon abides there, and broods the gold for 300 years.

Now a certain thrall, who had misdone against his lord and was fleeing from his wrath, haps on the said treasure and takes a cup thence, which

he brings to his lord to appease his wrath. The
Worm waketh, and findeth his treasure lessened,
but can find no man who hath done the deed.
Therefore he turns on the folk, and wars on
them, and burns Beowulf's house.

Now Beowulf will go and meet the Worm.
He has an iron shield made, and sets forth with
eleven men and the thrall the thirteenth. He
comes to the ness, and speaks to his men, telling
them of his past days, and gives them his last
greeting : then he cries out a challenge to the
Worm, who comes forth, and the battle begins :
Beowulf's sword will not bite on the Worm.
Wiglaf eggs on the others to come to Beowulf's
help, and goes himself straightway, and offers
himself to Beowulf; the Worm comes on again,
and Beowulf breaks his sword Nægling on him,
and the Worm wounds Beowulf. Wiglaf smites
the Worm in the belly; Beowulf draws his sax,
and between them they slay the Worm.

Beowulf now feels his wounds, and knows that
he is hurt deadly; he sits down by the wall, and
Wiglaf bathes his wounds. Beowulf speaks, tells
how he would give his armour to his son if he had
one; thanks God that he has not sworn falsely
or done guilefully; and prays Wiglaf to bear out
the treasure that he may see it before he dies.

Wiglaf fetches out the treasure, and again bathes Beowulf's wounds; Beowulf speaks again, rejoices over the sight of the treasure; gives to Wiglaf his ring and his armour, and bids the manner of his bale-fire. With that he passes away. Now the dastards come thereto and find Wiglaf vainly bathing his dead lord. He casteth shame upon them with great wrath. Thence he sends a messenger to the barriers of the town, who comes to the host, and tells them of the death of Beowulf. He tells withal of the old feud betwixt the Geats and the Swedes, and how these, when they hear of the death of the king, will be upon them. The warriors go to look on Beowulf, and find him and the Worm lying dead together. Wiglaf chooses out seven of them to go void the treasure-house, after having bidden them gather wood for the bale-fire. They shove the Worm over the cliff into the sea, and bear off the treasure in wains. Then they bring Beowulf's corpse to bale, and they kindle it; a woman called the wife of aforetime, it may be Hygd, widow of Hygelac, bemoans him: and twelve children of the athelings ride round the bale, and bemoan Beowulf and praise him: and thus ends the poem.

THE STORY OF BEOWULF

I. AND FIRST OF THE KINDRED OF HROTHGAR.

WHAT! we of the Spear-Danes of yore
 days, so was it
 That we learn'd of the fair fame of
 kings of the folks
And the athelings a-faring in framing of
 valour.
Oft then Scyld the Sheaf-son from the hosts of
 the scathers,
From kindreds a many the mead-settles tore;
It was then the earl fear'd them, sithence was he
 first
Found bare and all-lacking; so solace he bided,
Wax'd under the welkin in worship to thrive,
Until it was so that the round-about sitters
All over the whale-road must hearken his will   10
And yield him the tribute. A good king was
 that.

By whom then thereafter a son was begotten,
A youngling in garth, whom the great God sent
   thither
To foster the folk; and their crime-need he felt
The load that lay on them while lordless they
   lived
For a long while and long.   He therefore, the
   Life-lord,
The Wielder of glory, world's worship he gave him:
Brim Beowulf waxed, and wide the weal upsprang
Of the offspring of Scyld in the parts of the
   Scede-lands.
Such wise shall a youngling with wealth be
   a-working   20
With goodly fee-gifts toward the friends of his
   father,
That after in eld-days shall ever bide with him,
Fair fellows well-willing when wendeth the war-
   tide,
Their lief lord a-serving.   By praise-deeds it
   shall be
That in each and all kindreds a man shall have
   thriving.
   Then went his ways Scyld when the shapen
      while was,
All hardy to wend him to the lord and his
   warding:

Out then did they bear him to the side of the sea-
    flood,
The dear fellows of him, as he himself pray'd them
While yet his word wielded the friend of the
    Scyldings,   30
The dear lord of the land; a long while had he
    own'd it.
With stem all be-ringed at the hythe stood the ship,
All icy and out-fain, the Atheling's ferry.
There then did they lay him, the lord well be-
    loved,
The gold-rings' bestower, within the ship's barm,
The mighty by mast.   Much there was the
    treasure,
From far ways forsooth had the fret-work been led:
Never heard I of keel that was comelier dighted
With weapons of war, and with weed of the
    battle,
With bills and with byrnies.   There lay in his
    barm   40
Much wealth of the treasure that with him
    should be,
And he into the flood's might afar to depart.
No lesser a whit were the wealth-goods they dight
    him
Of the goods of the folk, than did they who
    aforetime,

When was the beginning, first sent him away
Alone o'er the billows, and he but a youngling.
   Moreover they set him up there a sign golden
High up overhead, and let the holm bear him,
Gave all to the Spearman.   Sad mind they had in
    them,
And mourning their mood was.   Now never knew
    men,   50
For sooth how to say it, rede-masters in hall,
Or heroes 'neath heaven, to whose hands came
    the lading.

II. CONCERNING HROTHGAR, AND HOW HE BUILT THE HOUSE CALLED HART. ALSO GRENDEL IS TOLD OF.

IN the burgs then was biding Beowulf the
    Scylding,
  Dear King of the people, for long was he
    dwelling
Far-famed of folks (his father turn'd elsewhere,
From his stead the Chief wended) till awoke to
    him after
Healfdene the high, and long while he held it,
Ancient and war-eager, o'er the glad Scyldings:
Of his body four bairns are forth to him rimed;
Into the world woke the leader of war-hosts   60

Heorogar; eke Hrothgar, and Halga the good;
Heard I that Elan queen was she of Ongentheow,
That Scylding of battle, the bed-mate behalsed.
    Then was unto Hrothgar the war-speed given,
Such worship of war that his kin and well-willers
Well hearken'd his will till the younglings were
    waxen,
A kin-host a many.   Then into his mind ran
That he would be building for him now a hall-
    house,
That men should be making a mead-hall more
    mighty
Than the children of ages had ever heard tell of: 70
And there within eke should he be out-dealing
To young and to old all things God had given,
Save the share of the folk and the life-days of men.
Then heard I that widely the work was a-banning
To kindreds a many the Middle-garth over
To fret o'er that folk-stead. So befell to him timely
Right soon among men that made was it yarely
The most of hall-houses, and Hart its name shap'd
    he,
Who wielded his word full widely around.
His behest he belied not; it was he dealt the
    rings,   80
The wealth at the high-tide. Then up rose the
    hall-house,

High up and horn-gabled.   Hot surges it bided
Of fire-flame the loathly, nor long was it thence-
     forth
Ere sorely the edge-hate 'twixt Son and Wife's
     Father
After the slaughter-strife there should awaken.
     Then the ghost heavy-strong bore with it hardly
E'en for a while of time, bider in darkness,
That there on each day of days heard he the
     mirth-tide
Loud in the hall-house. There was the harp's voice,
And clear song of shaper.   Said he who could it 90
To tell the first fashion of men from aforetime;
Quoth how the Almighty One made the Earth's
     fashion,
The fair field and bright midst the bow of the
     Waters,
And with victory beglory'd set Sun and Moon,
Bright beams to enlighten the biders on land:
And how he adorned all parts of the earth
With limbs and with leaves; and life withal shaped
For the kindred of each thing that quick on earth
     wendeth.
     So liv'd on all happy the host of the kinsmen
In game and in glee, until one wight began,   100
A fiend out of hell-pit, the framing of evil,
And Grendel forsooth the grim guest was hight,

The mighty mark-strider, the holder of moorland,
The fen and the fastness. The stead of the fifel
That wight all unhappy a while of time warded,
Sithence that the Shaper him had for-written.

   On the kindred of Cain the Lord living ever
Awreaked the murder of the slaying of Abel.
In that feud he rejoic'd not, but afar him He
   banish'd,
The Maker, from mankind for the crime he had
   wrought.   110
But offspring uncouth thence were they awoken
Eotens and elf-wights, and ogres of ocean,
And therewith the Giants, who won war against
   God
A long while; but He gave them their wages
   therefor.

III. HOW GRENDEL FELL UPON HART AND WASTED IT.

NOW went he a-spying, when come was the
   night-tide,
   The house on high builded, and how there
   the Ring-Danes
Their beer-drinking over had boune them to bed;
And therein he found them, the atheling fellows,
Asleep after feasting. Then sorrow they knew not

Nor the woe of mankind: but the wight of
    wealth's waning,   120
The grim and the greedy, soon yare was he gotten,
All furious and fierce, and he raught up from
    resting
A thirty of thanes, and thence aback got him
Right fain of his gettings, and homeward to fare,
Fulfilled of slaughter his stead to go look on.
    Thereafter at dawning, when day was yet early,
The war-craft of Grendel to men grew unhidden,
And after his meal was the weeping uphoven,
Mickle voice of the morning-tide: there the
    Prince mighty,
The Atheling exceeding good, unblithe he sat, 130
Tholing the heavy woe; thane-sorrow dreed he
Since the slot of the loathly wight there they had
    look'd on,
The ghost all accursed.   O'er grisly the strife was,
So loathly and longsome.   No longer the frist was
But after the wearing of one night; then fram'd he
Murder-bales more yet, and nowise he mourned
The feud and the crime; over fast therein was he.
Then easy to find was the man who would else-
    where
Seek out for himself a rest was more roomsome,
Beds end-long the bowers, when beacon'd to him
    was,   140

And soothly out told by manifest token,
The hate of the hell-thane. He held himself
    sithence
Further and faster who from the fiend gat him.
  In such wise he rul'd it and wrought against
    right,
But one against all, until idle was standing
The best of hall-houses; and mickle the while was,
Twelve winter-tides' wearing; and trouble he
    tholed,
That friend of the Scyldings, of woes every one
And wide-spreading sorrows : for sithence it fell
That unto men's children unbidden 'twas known
Full sadly in singing, that Grendel won war   151
'Gainst Hrothgar a while of time, hate-envy
    waging,
And crime-guilts and feud for seasons no few,
And strife without stinting. For the sake of no
    kindness
Unto any of men of the main-host of Dane-folk
Would he thrust off the life-bale, or by fee-gild
    allay it,
Nor was there a wise man that needed to ween
The bright boot to have at the hand of the slayer.
The monster the fell one afflicted them sorely,
That death-shadow darksome the doughty and
    youthful   160

Enfetter'd, ensnared; night by night was he
    faring
The moorlands the misty.   But never know men
Of spell-workers of Hell to and fro where they
    wander.
So crime-guilts a many the foeman of mankind,
The fell alone-farer, fram'd oft and full often,
Cruel hard shames and wrongful, and Hart he
    abode in,
The treasure-stain'd hall, in the dark of the night-
    tide;
But never the gift-stool therein might he greet,
The treasure before the Creator he trow'd not.
  Mickle wrack was it soothly for the friend of
    the Scyldings,   170
Yea heart and mood breaking.   Now sat there a
    many
Of the mighty in rune, and won them the rede
Of what thing for the strong-soul'd were best of
    all things
Which yet they might frame 'gainst the fear and
    the horror.
And whiles they behight them at the shrines of
    the heathen
To worship the idols; and pray'd they in words,
That he, the ghost-slayer, would frame for them
    helping

'Gainst the folk-threats and evil. So far'd they
    their wont,
The hope of the heathen; nor hell they remember'd
In mood and in mind. And the Maker they
    knew not,   180
The Doomer of deeds: nor of God the Lord
    wist they,
Nor the Helm of the Heavens knew aught how
    to hery,
The Wielder of Glory. Woe worth unto that man
Who through hatred the baneful his soul shall
    shove into
The fire's embrace ; nought of fostering weens he,
Nor of changing one whit. But well is he soothly
That after the death-day shall seek to the Lord,
In the breast of the Father all peace ever craving.

IV. NOW COMES BEOWULF ECG-THEOW'S SON TO THE LAND OF THE DANES, AND THE WALL-WARDEN SPEAKETH WITH HIM.

SO care that was time-long the kinsman of
    Healfdene
    Still seeth'd without ceasing, nor might the
    wise warrior   190
Wend otherwhere woe, for o'er strong was the strife

All loathly so longsome late laid on the people,
Need-wrack and grim nithing, of night-bales the
    greatest.
    Now that from his home heard the Hygelac's
    thane,
Good midst of the Geat-folk; of Grendel's deeds
    heard he.
But he was of mankind of might and main
    mightiest
In the day that we tell of, the day of this life,
All noble, strong-waxen.   He bade a wave-
    wearer
Right good to be gear'd him, and quoth he that
    the war-king
Over the swan-road he would be seeking,   200
The folk-lord far-famed, since lack of men had he.
Forsooth of that faring the carles wiser-fashion'd
Laid little blame on him, though lief to them
    was he;
The heart-hardy whetted they, heeded the omen.
There had the good one, e'en he of the Geat-folk,
Champions out-chosen of them that he keenest
Might find for his needs; and he then the
    fifteenth
Sought to the sound-wood.   A swain thereon
    show'd him,
A sea-crafty man, all the make of the land-marks.

Wore then a while, on the waves was the
    floater,   210
The boat under the berg, and yare then the
    warriors
Strode up on the stem ; the streams were a-winding
The sea 'gainst the sands. Upbore the swains then
Up into the bark's barm the bright-fretted
    weapons,
The war-array stately; then out the lads shov'd her,
The folk on the welcome way shov'd out the
    wood-bound.
Then by the wind driven out o'er the wave-holm
Far'd the foamy-neck'd floater most like to a fowl,
Till when was the same tide of the second day's
    wearing
The wound-about-stemm'd one had waded her way,
So that then they that sail'd her had sight of the
    land,   221
Bleak shine of the sea-cliffs, bergs steep up above,
Sea-nesses wide reaching ; the sound was won over,
The sea-way was ended : then up ashore swiftly
The band of the Weder-folk up on earth wended ;
They bound up the sea-wood, their sarks on them
    rattled,
Their weed of the battle, and God there they
    thanked
For that easy the wave-ways were waxen unto them.

But now from the wall saw the Scylding-folks'
    warder,
E'en he who the holm-cliffs should ever be holding,
Men bear o'er the gangway the bright shields
    a-shining,   231
Folk-host gear all ready. Then mind-longing
    wore him,
And stirr'd up his mood to wot who were the
    men-folk.
So shoreward down far'd he his fair steed a-riding,
Hrothgar's Thane, and full strongly then set he
    a-quaking
The stark wood in his hands, and in council-
    speech speer'd he :
    What men be ye then of them that have war-
        gear,
With byrnies bewarded, who the keel high up-
    builded
Over the Lake-street thus have come leading,
Hither o'er holm-ways hieing in ring-stem ?   240
End-sitter was I, a-holding the sea-ward,
That the land of the Dane-folk none of the
    loathly
Faring with ship-horde ever might scathe it.
None yet have been seeking more openly hither
Of shield-havers than ye, and ye of the leave-word
Of the framers of war naught at all wotting,

Or the manners of kinsmen.   But no man of earls
   greater
Saw I ever on earth than one of you yonder,
The warrior in war-gear : no hall-man, so ween I,
Is that weapon-beworthy'd, but his visage belie
   him,   250
The sight seen once only.   Now I must be
   wotting
The spring of your kindred ere further ye cast ye,
And let loose your false spies in the Dane-land
   a-faring
Yet further afield.   So now, ye far-dwellers,
Ye wenders o'er sea-flood, this word do ye hearken
Of my one-folded thought : and haste is the
   handiest
To do me to wit of whence is your coming.

V. HERE BEOWULF MAKES ANSWER TO THE LAND-WARDEN, WHO SHOW-ETH HIM THE WAY TO THE KING'S ABODE.

HE then that was chiefest in thus wise he
   answer'd,
   The war-fellows' leader unlock'd he the
   word-hoard :
We be a people of the Weder-Geats' man-kin   260

And of Hygelac be we the hearth-fellows soothly.
My father before me of folks was well-famed
Van-leader and atheling, Ecgtheow he hight.
Many winters abode he, and on the way wended
An old man from the garths, and him well re-
    members
Every wise man well nigh wide yond o'er the
    earth.
Through our lief mood and friendly the lord
    that is thine,
Even Healfdene's son, are we now come a-seeking,
Thy warder of folk. Learn us well with thy
    leading,
For we have to the mighty an errand full mickle,
To the lord of the Dane-folk: naught dark
    shall it be,   271
That ween I full surely. If it be so thou wottest,
As soothly for our parts we now have heard say,
That one midst of the Scyldings, who of scathers
    I wot not,
A deed-hater secret, in the dark of the night-tide
Setteth forth through the terror the malice un-
    told of,
The shame-wrong and slaughter. I therefore to
    Hrothgar
Through my mind fashion'd roomsome the rede
    may now learn him,

How he, old-wise and good, may get the fiend
    under,
If once more from him awayward may turn   280
The business of bales, and the boot come again,
And the weltering of care wax cooler once more;
Or for ever sithence time of stress he shall thole,
The need and the wronging, the while yet there
    abideth
On the high stead aloft the best of all houses.
    Then spake out the warden on steed there
        a-sitting,
The servant all un-fear'd: It shall be of either
That the shield-warrior sharp the sundering
    wotteth,
Of words and of works, if he think thereof well.
I hear it thus said that this host here is friendly 290
To the lord of the Scyldings; forth fare ye then,
    bearing
Your weed and your weapons, of the way will I
    wise you;
Likewise mine own kinsmen I will now be bidding
Against every foeman your floater before us,
Your craft but new-tarred, the keel on the sand,
With honour to hold, until back shall be bearing
Over the lake-streams this one, the lief man,
The wood of the wounden-neck back unto
    Wedermark.

Unto such shall be granted amongst the good-
    doers   299
To win the way out all whole from the war-race.
Then boun they to faring, the bark biding quiet;
Hung upon hawser the wide-fathom'd ship
Fast at her anchor.   Forth shone the boar-shapes
Over the check-guards golden adorned,
Fair-shifting, fire-hard; ward held the farrow.
Snorted the war-moody, hasten'd the warriors
And trod down together until the hall timber'd,
Stately and gold-bestain'd, gat they to look on,
That was the all-mightiest unto earth's dwellers
Of halls 'neath the heavens, wherein bode the
    mighty;   310
Glisten'd the gleam thereof o'er lands a many.
Unto them then the war-deer the court of the
    proud one
Full clearly betaught it, that they therewithal
Might wend their ways thither.   Then he of the
    warriors
Round wended his steed, and spake a word back-
    ward:
Time now for my faring; but the Father All-
    wielder
May He with all helping henceforward so hold you
All whole in your wayfaring.   Will I to sea-side
Against the wroth folk to hold warding ever.

VI. BEOWULF AND THE GEATS COME INTO HART.

STONE-DIVERSE the street was, straight
    uplong the path led   320
  The warriors together. There shone the war-
    byrny
The hard and the hand-lock'd ; the ring-iron sheer
Sang over their war-gear, when they ᵗᵒ the hall
    first
In their gear the all-fearful had gat them to
    ganging.
So then the sea-weary their wide shields set down,
Their war-rounds the mighty, against the hall's
    wall.
Then bow'd they to bench, and rang there the
    byrnies,
The war-weed of warriors, and up-stood the spears,
The war-gear of the sea-folk all gather'd together,
The ash-holt grey-headed ; that host of the
    iron   330
With weapons was worshipful. There then a
    proud chief
Of those lads of the battle speer'd after their line :
  Whence ferry ye then the shields golden-faced,
The grey sarks therewith, and the helms all be-
    visor'd,

And a heap of the war-shafts? Now am I of Hrothgar
The man and the messenger : ne'er saw I of aliens
So many of men more might-like of mood.
I ween that for pride-sake, no wise for wrack-
    wending
But for high might of mind, ye to Hrothgar have
    sought.
    Unto him then the heart-hardy answer'd and
        spake,   340
The proud earl of the Weders the word gave
    aback,
The hardy neath helm : Now of Hygelac are we
The board-fellows ; Beowulf e'en is my name,
And word will I say unto Healfdene's son,
To the mighty, the folk-lord, what errand is mine,
Yea unto thy lord, if to us he will grant it
That him, who so good is, anon we may greet.
    Spake Wulfgar the word, a lord of the
        Wendels,
And the mood of his heart of a many was kenned,
His war and his wisdom : I therefore the Danes'
    friend   350
Will lightly be asking, of the lord of the
    Scyldings,
The dealer of rings, since the boon thou art
    bidding,

The mighty folk-lord, concerning thine errand,
And swiftly the answer shall do thee to wit
Which the good one to give thee aback may
    deem meetest.
    Then turn'd he in haste to where Hrothgar
    was sitting
Right old and all hoary mid the host of his earl-
    folk :
Went the valour-stark ; stood he the shoulders
    before
Of the Dane-lord : well could he the doughty
    ones' custom.
So Wulfgar spake forth to his lord the well-
    friendly :   360
Hither are ferry'd now, come from afar off
O'er the field of the ocean, a folk of the Geats ;
These men of the battle e'en Beowulf name they
Their elder and chiefest, and to thee are they
    bidding
That they, O dear lord, with thee may be dealing
In word against word. Now win them no naysay
Of thy speech again-given, O Hrothgar the glad-
    man :
For they in their war-gear, methinketh, be worthy
Of good deeming of earls ; and forsooth naught
    but doughty
Is he who hath led o'er the warriors hither.   370

VII. BEOWULF SPEAKETH WITH HROTHGAR, AND TELLETH HOW HE WILL MEET GRENDEL.

WORD then gave out Hrothgar the helm
    of the Scyldings:
    I knew him in sooth when he was but a
        youngling,
And his father, the old man, was Ecgtheow hight;
Unto whom at his home gave Hrethel the Geat-
    lord
His one only daughter; and now hath his off-
    spring
All hardy come hither a lief lord to seek him.
For that word they spake then, the sea-faring men,
E'en they who the gift-scat for the Geat-folk had
    ferry'd,
Brought thither for thanks, that of thirty of men-
    folk
The craft of might hath he within his own hand-
    grip,   380
That war-strong of men.   Now him holy God
For kind help hath sent off here even to us,
We men of the West Danes, as now I have
    weening,
'Gainst the terror of Grendel.   So I to that good
    one

For his mighty mood-daring shall the dear trea-
    sure bid.
Haste now and be speedy, and bid them in
    straightway,
The kindred-band gather'd together, to see us,
And in words say thou eke that they be well
    comen
To the folk of the Danes. To the door of the
    hall then
Went Wulfgar, and words withinward he
    flitted :   390
    He bade me to say you, my lord of fair
    battle,
The elder of East-Danes, that he your blood
    knoweth,
And that unto him are ye the sea-surges over,
Ye lads hardy-hearted, well come to land hither ;
And now may ye wend you all in war-raiment
Under the battle-mask Hrothgar to see.
But here let your battle-boards yet be abiding,
With your war-weed and slaughter-shafts, issue
    of words.
    Then rose up the rich one, much warriors
    around him,
Chosen heap of the thanes, but there some abided
The war-gear to hold, as the wight one was
    bidding.   401

Swift went they together, as the warrior there
    led them,
Under Hart's roof : went the stout-hearted,
The hardy neath helm, till he stood by the high-
    seat.
Then Beowulf spake out, on him shone the byrny,
His war-net besown by the wiles of the smith :
    Hail to thee, Hrothgar ! I am of Hygelac
Kinsman and folk-thane ; fair deeds have I many
Begun in my youth-tide, and this matter of Gren-
    del   409
On the turf of mine own land undarkly I knew.
'Tis the seafarers' say that standeth this hall,
The best house forsooth, for each one of warriors
All idle and useless, after the even-light
Under the heaven-loft hidden becometh.
Then lightly they learn'd me, my people, this
    lore,
E'en the best that there be of the wise of the
    churls,
O Hrothgar the kingly, that thee should I seek to,
Whereas of the might of my craft were they
    cunning ;
For they saw me when came I from out of my
    wargear,
Blood-stain'd from the foe whenas five had I
    bounden,   420

Quell'd the kin of the eotens, and in the wave
    slain
The nicors by night-tide : strait need then I bore,
Wreak'd the grief of the Weders, the woe they
    had gotten ;
I ground down the wrathful ; and now against
    Grendel
I here with the dread one alone shall be dooming,
In Thing with the giant.   I now then with thee,
O lord of the bright Danes, will fall to my
    bidding,
O berg of Scyldings, and bid thee one boon,
Which, O refuge of warriors, gainsay me not now,
Since, O free friend of folks, from afar have I
    come,   430
 That I alone, I and my band of the earls,
This hard heap of men, may cleanse Hart of ill.
This eke have I heard say, that he, the fell
    monster,
In his wan-heed recks nothing of weapons of war ;
Forgo I this therefore (if so be that Hygelac
Will still be my man-lord, and he blithe of
    mood)
To bear the sword with me, or bear the broad
    shield,
Yellow-round to the battle ; but with naught save
    the hand-grip

With the foe shall I grapple, and grope for the
  life
The loathly with loathly.   There he shall believe
In the doom of the Lord whom death then shall
  take.   441
Now ween I that he, if he may wield matters,
E'en there in the war-hall the folk of the Geats
Shall eat up unafear'd, as oft he hath done it
With the might of the Hrethmen: no need for
  thee therefore
My head to be hiding; for me will he have
With gore all bestain'd, if the death of men get
  me;
He will bear off my bloody corpse minded to
  taste it;
Unmournfully then will the Lone-goer eat it,
Will blood-mark the moor-ways; for the meat
  of my body   450
Naught needest thou henceforth in any wise
  grieve thee.
But send thou to Hygelac, if the war have me,
The best of all war-shrouds that now my breast
  wardeth,
The goodliest of railings, the good gift of
  Hrethel,
The hand-work of Weland.   Weird wends as she
  willeth.

VIII. HROTHGAR ANSWERETH BEO-
WULF AND BIDDETH HIM SIT TO
THE FEAST.

SPAKE out then Hrothgar the helm of the
Scyldings :
Thou Beowulf, friend mine, for battle that
wardeth
And for help that is kindly hast sought to us
hither.
Fought down thy father the most of all feuds ;
To Heatholaf was he forsooth for a hand-bane 460
Amidst of the Wylfings. The folk of the
Weders
Him for the war-dread that while might not
hold.
So thence did he seek to the folk of the South-
Danes
O'er the waves' wallow, to the Scyldings be-
worshipp'd.
Then first was I wielding the weal of the Dane-
folk,
That time was I holding in youth-tide the gem-
rich
Hoard-burg of the heroes. Dead then was
Heorogar,
Mine elder of brethren ; unliving was he,

The Healfdene's bairn that was better than I.
That feud then thereafter with fee did I settle; 470
I sent to the Wylfing folk over the waters' back
Treasures of old time; he swore the oaths
    to me.
Sorrow is in my mind that needs must I say it
To any of grooms, of Grendel what hath he
Of shaming in Hart, and he with his hate-wiles
Of sudden harms framed; the host of my hall-
    floor,
The war-heap, is waned; Weird swept them away
Into horror of Grendel.   It is God now that
    may lightly
The scather the doltish from deeds thrust aside.
Full oft have they boasted with beer well be-
    drunken,   480
My men of the battle all over the ale-stoup,
That they in the beer-hall would yet be abiding
The onset of Grendel with the terror of edges.
But then was this mead-hall in the tide of the
    morning,
This warrior-hall, gore-stain'd when day at last
    gleamed,
All the boards of the benches with blood be-
    steam'd over,
The hall laid with sword-gore: of lieges less
    had I

Of dear and of doughty, for them death had
    gotten.
Now sit thou to feast and unbind thy mood
    freely,
Thy war-fame unto men as the mind of thee
    whetteth.   490
  Then was for the Geat-folk and them all
    together
There in the beer-hall a bench bedight roomsome,
There the stout-hearted hied them to sitting
Proud in their might : a thane minded the service,
Who in hand upbare an ale-stoup adorned,
Skinked the sheer mead ; whiles sang the shaper
Clear out in Hart-hall ; joy was of warriors,
Men doughty no little of Danes and of Weders.

IX. UNFERTH CONTENDETH IN WORDS WITH BEOWULF.

SPAKE out then Unferth that bairn was of
    Ecglaf,
  And he sat at the feet of the lord of the
    Scyldings,   500
He unbound the battle-rune ; was Beowulf's
    faring,
Of him the proud mere-farer, mickle unliking,
Whereas he begrudg'd it of any man other

That he glories more mighty the middle-garth
    over
Should hold under heaven than he himself held:
    Art thou that Beowulf who won strife with
    Breca
On the wide sea contending in swimming,
When ye two for pride's sake search'd out the
    floods
And for a dolt's cry into deep water
Thrust both your life-days? No man the twain
    of you,   510
Lief or loth were he, might lay wyte to stay you
Your sorrowful journey, when on the sea row'd ye;
Then when the ocean-stream ye with your arms
    deck'd,
Meted the mere-streets, there your hands bran-
    dish'd!
O'er the Spearman ye glided; the sea with waves
    welter'd,
The surge of the winter. Ye twain in the waves'
    might
For a seven nights swink'd. He outdid thee in
    swimming,
And the more was his might; but him in the
    morn-tide
To the Heatho-Remes' land the holm bore
    ashore,

And thence away sought he to his dear land and
    lovely,   520
The lief to his people sought the land of the
    Brondings,
The fair burg peace-warding, where he the folk
    owned,
The burg and the gold rings. What to thee-
    ward he boasted,
Beanstan's son, for thee soothly he brought it
    about.
Now ween I for thee things worser than erewhile,
Though thou in the war-race wert everywhere
    doughty,
In the grim war, if thou herein Grendel darest
Night-long for a while of time nigh to abide.
    Then Beowulf spake out, the Ecgtheow's bairn :
What ! thou no few of things, O Unferth my
    friend,   530
And thou drunken with beer, about Breca hast
    spoken,
Saidest out of his journey; so the sooth now I tell :
To wit, that the more might ever I owned,
Hard wearing on wave more than any man else.
We twain then, we quoth it, while yet we were
    younglings,
And we boasted between us, the twain of us being
    yet

In our youth-days, that we out onto the Spearman
Our lives would adventure ; and e'en so we
    wrought it.
We had a sword naked, when on the sound row'd
    we,   539
Hard in hand, as we twain against the whale-fishes
Had mind to be warding us.   No whit from me
In the waves of the sea-flood afar might he float
The hastier in holm, nor would I from him hie me.
Then we two together, we were in the sea
For a five nights, till us twain the flood drave
    asunder,
The weltering of waves.   Then the coldest of
    weathers
In the dusking of night and the wind from the
    northward
Battle-grim turn'd against us, rough grown were
    the billows.
Of the mere-fishes then was the mood all up-
    stirred ;
There me 'gainst the loathly the body-sark mine,
The hard and the hand-lock'd, was framing me
    help,   551
My battle-rail braided, it lay on my breast
Gear'd graithly with gold.   But me to the ground
    tugg'd
A foe and fiend-scather ; fast he had me in hold

That grim one in grip: yet to me was it given,
That the wretch there, the monster, with point
    might I reach,
With my bill of the battle, and the war-race off
    bore
The mighty mere-beast through the hand that
    was mine.

X. BEOWULF MAKES AN END OF HIS TALE OF THE SWIMMING. WEALH-THEOW, HROTHGAR'S QUEEN, GREETS HIM; AND HROTHGAR DELIVERS TO HIM THE WARDING OF THE HALL.

THUS oft and oft over the doers of evil
    They threaten'd me hard; thane-service I
    did them   560
With the dear sword of mine, as forsooth it was
    meet,
That nowise of their fill did they win them the joy
The evil fordoers in swallowing me down,
Sitting round at the feast nigh the ground of the
    sea.
Yea rather, a morning-tide, mangled by sword-edge
Along the waves' leaving up there did they lie
Lull'd asleep with the sword, so that never
    sithence

c

About the deep floods for the farers o'er ocean
The way have they letted.   Came the light from
    the eastward,   569
The bright beacon of God, and grew the seas calm,
So that the sea-nesses now might I look on,
The windy walls.   Thuswise Weird oft will be
    saving
The earl that is unfey, when his valour availeth.
Whatever, it happ'd me that I with the sword slew
Nicors nine.   Never heard I of fighting a night-
    tide
'Neath the vault of the heavens was harder than
    that,
Nor yet on the sea-streams of woefuller wight.
Whatever, forth won I with life from the foes'
    clutch
All of wayfaring weary.   But me the sea upbore,
The flood downlong the tide with the weltering
    of waters,   580
All onto the Finnland.   No whit of thee ever
Mid such strife of the battle-gear have I heard say,
Such terrors of bills.   Nor never yet Breca
In the play of the battle, nor both you, nor either,
So dearly the deeds have framed forsooth
With the bright flashing swords ; though of this
    naught I boast me.
But thou of thy brethren the banesman becamest,

Yea thine head-kin forsooth, for which in hell
    shalt thou
Dree weird of damnation, though doughty thy
    wit be ;
For unto thee say I forsooth, son of Ecglaf,   590
That so many deeds never Grendel had done,
That monster the loathly, against thine own lord,
The shaming in Hart-hall, if suchwise thy mind
    were,
And thy soul e'en as battle-fierce, such as thou
    sayest.
But he, he hath fram'd it that the feud he may
    heed not,
The fearful edge-onset that is of thy folk,
Nor sore need be fearful of the Victory-Scyldings.
The need-pledges taketh he, no man he spareth
Of the folk of the Danes, driveth war as he lusteth,
Slayeth and feasteth unweening of strife   600
With them of the Spear-Danes. But I, I shall
    show it,
The Geats' wightness and might ere the time
    weareth old,
Shall bide him in war-tide. Then let him go who
    may go
High-hearted to mead, sithence when the morn-
    light
O'er the children of men of the second day hence,

The sun clad in heaven's air, shines from the
    southward.

   Then merry of heart was the meter of treasures,
The hoary-man'd war-renown'd, help now he
    trow'd in;
The lord of the Bright-Danes on Beowulf
    hearken'd,   609
The folk-shepherd knew him, his fast-ready mind.
There was laughter of heroes, and high the din rang
And winsome the words were. Went Wealhtheow
    forth,
The Queen she of Hrothgar, of courtesies mindful,
The gold-array'd greeted the grooms in the hall,
The free and frank woman the beaker there wended,
And first to the East-Dane-folk's fatherland's
    warder,
And bade him be blithe at the drinking of beer,
To his people beloved, and lustily took he
The feast and the hall-cup, that victory-fam'd
    King.
Then round about went she, the Dame of the
    Helmings,   620
And to doughty and youngsome, each deal of the
    folk there,
Gave cups of the treasure, till now it betid
That to Beowulf duly the Queen the ring-dighted,
Of mind high uplifted, the mead-beaker bare.

Then she greeted the Geat-lord, and gave God
    the thank,
She, the wisefast in words, that the will had wax'd
    in her
In one man of the earls to have trusting and troth
For comfort from crimes.   But the cup then he
    took,
The slaughter-fierce warrior, from Wealhtheow
    the Queen.   629
And then rim'd he the word, making ready for war,
And Beowulf spake forth, the Ecgtheow's bairn :
  E'en that in mind had I when up on holm
    strode I,
And in sea-boat sat down with a band of my
    men,
That for once and for all the will of your people
Would I set me to work, or. on slaughter-field
    cringe
Fast in grip of the fiend ; yea and now shall I
    frame
The valour of earl-folk, or else be abiding
The day of mine end, here down in the mead-hall.
  To the wife those his words well liking they
    were,
The big word of the Geat; and the gold-adorn'd
    wended,   640
The frank and free Queen to sit by her lord.

And thereafter within the high hall was as erst
The proud word outspoken and bliss on the people,
Was the sound of the victory-folk, till on a sudden
The Healfdene's son would now be a-seeking
His rest of the even : wotted he for the Evil
Within the high hall was the Hild-play bedight,
Sithence that the sun-light no more should they see,
When night should be darkening, and down
    over all
The shapes of the shadow-helms should be
    a-striding   650
Wan under the welkin. Uprose then all war-folk ;
Then greeted the glad-minded one man the other,
Hrothgar to Beowulf, bidding him hail,
And the wine-hall to wield, and withal quoth the
    word :
    Never to any man erst have I given,
Since the hand and the shield's round aloft might
    I heave,
This high hall of the Dane-folk, save now unto
    thee.
Have now and hold the best of all houses,
Mind thee of fame, show the might of thy valour !
Wake the wroth one : no lack shall there be to
    thy willing   660
If that wight work thou win and life there-
    withal.

XI. NOW IS BEOWULF LEFT IN THE HALL ALONE WITH HIS MEN.

THEN wended him Hrothgar with the
band of his warriors,
  The high-ward of the Scyldings from out
    of the hall,
For then would the war-lord go seek unto Wealh-
  theow
The Queen for a bed-mate. The glory of king-
  folk
Against Grendel had set, as men have heard say,
A hall-ward who held him a service apart
In the house of the Dane-lord, for eoten-ward
  held he.
Forsooth he, the Geat-lord, full gladly he trowed
In the might of his mood and the grace of the
  Maker.   670
Therewith he did off him his byrny of iron
And the helm from his head, and his dighted
  sword gave,
The best of all irons, to the thane that abode
  him,
And bade him to hold that harness of battle.
Bespake then the good one, a big word he gave
  out,
Beowulf the Geat, ere on the bed strode he :

Nowise in war I deem me more lowly
In the works of the battle than Grendel, I ween;
So not with the sword shall I lull him to
    slumber,
Or take his life thuswise, though to me were it
    easy;   680
Of that good wise he wots not, to get the stroke
    on me,
To hew on my shield, for as stark as he shall be
In the works of the foeman. So we twain a
    night-tide
Shall forgo the sword, if he dare yet to seek
The war without weapons. Sithence the wise
    God,
The Lord that is holy, on which hand soever
The glory may doom as due to him seemeth.
    Bowed down then the war-deer, the cheek-
    bolster took
The face of the earl; and about him a many
Of sea-warriors bold to their hall-slumber bow'd
    them;   690
No one of them thought that thence away should
    he
Seek ever again to his home the beloved,
His folk or his free burg, where erst he was fed;
For of men had they learn'd that o'er mickle a
    many

In that wine-hall aforetime the fell death had
    gotten
Of the folk of the Danes; but the Lord to them
    gave it,
To the folk of the Weders, the web of war-
    speeding,
Help fair and good comfort, e'en so that their
    foeman
Through the craft of one man all they over-
    came,
By the self-might of one.   So is manifest
    truth   700
That God the Almighty the kindred of men
Hath wielded wide ever.   Now by wan night
    there came,
There strode in the shade-goer; slept there the
    shooters,
They who that horn-house should be a-holding,
All men but one man: to men was that
    known,
That them indeed might not, since will'd not the
    Maker,
The scather unceasing drag off 'neath the
    shadow;
But he ever watching in wrath 'gainst the wroth
    one
Mood-swollen abided the battle-mote ever.

XII. GRENDEL COMETH INTO HART: OF THE STRIFE BETWIXT HIM AND BEOWULF.

CAME then from the moor-land, all under
    the mist-bents,   710
    Grendel a-going there, bearing God's anger.
The scather the ill one was minded of mankind
To have one in his toils from the high hall aloft.
'Neath the welkin he waded, to the place whence
    the wine-house,
The gold-hall of men, most yarely he wist
With gold-plates fair colour'd; nor was it the
    first time
That he unto Hrothgar's high home had betook
    him.
Never he in his life-days, either erst or there-
    after,
Of warriors more hardy or hall-thanes had found.
Came then to the house the wight on his ways, 720
Of all joys bereft; and soon sprang the door
    open,
With fire-bands made fast, when with hand he
    had touch'd it;
Brake the bale-heedy, he with wrath bollen,
The mouth of the house there, and early there-
    after

On the shiny-fleck'd floor thereof trod forth the
    fiend;
On went he then mood-wroth, and out from his
    eyes stood
Likest to fire-flame light full unfair.
In the high house beheld he a many of warriors,
A host of men sib all sleeping together,
Of man-warriors a heap; then laugh'd out his
    mood;   730
In mind deem'd he to sunder, or ever came day,
The monster, the fell one, from each of the men
    there
The life from the body; for befell him a boding
Of fulfilment of feeding: but weird now it was
    not
That he any more of mankind thenceforward
Should eat, that night over. Huge evil beheld
    then
The Hygelac's kinsman, and how the foul scather
All with his fear-grips would fare there before
    him;
How never the monster was minded to tarry,
For speedily gat he, and at the first stour,   740
A warrior a-sleeping, and unaware slit him,
Bit his bone-coffer, drank blood a-streaming,
Great gobbets swallow'd in; thenceforth soon
    had he

Of the unliving one every whit eaten
To hands and feet even: then forth strode he
    nigher,
And took hold with his hand upon him the high-
    hearted,
The warrior a-resting; reach'd out to himwards
The fiend with his hand, gat fast on him rathely
With thought of all evil, and besat him his arm.
Then swiftly was finding the herdsman of foul
    deeds   750
That forsooth he had met not in Middle-garth
    ever,
In the parts of the earth, in any man else
A hand-grip more mighty; then wax'd he of
    mood
Heart-fearful, but none the more outward might
    he;
Hence-eager his heart was to the darkness to hie
    him,
And the devil-dray seek: not there was his service
E'en such as he found in his life-days before.
Then to heart laid the good one, the Hygelac's
    kinsman,
His speech of the even-tide; uplong he stood
And fast with him grappled, till bursted his
    fingers.   760
The eoten was out-fain, but on strode the earl.

The mighty fiend minded was, whereso he might,
To wind him about more widely away thence,
And flee fenwards; he found then the might of
    his fingers
In the grip of the fierce one; sorry faring was
    that
Which he, the harm-scather, had taken to Hart.
The warrior-hall dinn'd now; unto all Danes
    there waxed,
To the castle-abiders, to each of the keen ones,
To all earls, as an ale-dearth.   Now angry were
    both
Of the fierce mighty warriors, far rang out the
    hall-house;   770
Then mickle the wonder it was that the wine-hall
Withstood the two war-deer, nor welter'd to earth
The fair earthly dwelling; but all fast was it
    builded
Within and without with the banding of iron
By crafty thought smithy'd.   But there from the
    sill bow'd
Fell many a mead-bench, by hearsay of mine,
With gold well adorned, where strove they the
    wrothful.
Hereof never ween'd they, the wise of the Scyld-
    ings,
That ever with might should any of men

The excellent, bone-dight, break into pieces,   780
Or unlock with cunning, save the light fire's
    embracing
In smoke should it swallow. So uprose the roar
New and enough ; now fell on the North-Danes
Ill fear and the terror, on each and on all men,
Of them who from wall-top hearken'd the weeping,
Even God's foeman singing the fear-lay,
The triumphless song, and the wound-bewailing
Of the thrall of the Hell ; for there now fast held
    him
He who of men of main was the mightiest
In that day which is told of, the day of this life.

XIII. BEOWULF HATH THE VICTORY : GRENDEL IS HURT DEADLY AND LEAVETH HAND AND ARM IN THE HALL.

NAUGHT would the earls' help for any-
    thing thenceforth   791
    That murder-comer yet quick let loose of,
Nor his life-days forsooth to any of folk
Told he for useful. Out then drew full many
Of Beowulf's earls the heir-loom of old days,
For their lord and their master's fair life would
    they ward,

That mighty of princes, if so might they do it.
For this did they know not when they the strife
    dreed,
Those hardy-minded men of the battle,
And on every half there thought to be hewing,   800
And search out his soul, that the ceaseless scather
Not any on earth of the choice of all irons,
Not one of the war-bills, would greet home for
    ever.
For he had forsworn him from victory-weapons,
And each one of edges.   But his sundering of soul
In the days that we tell of, the day of this life,
Should be weary and woeful, the ghost wending
    elsewhere
To the wielding of fiends to wend him afar.
Then found he out this, he who mickle erst made
Out of mirth of his mood unto children of men 810
And had fram'd many crimes, he the foeman of
    God,
That the body of him would not bide to avail
    him,
But the hardy of mood, even Hygelac's kinsman,
Had him fast by the hand : now was each to the
    other
All loathly while living : his body-sore bided
The monster : was manifest now on his shoulder
The unceasing wound, sprang the sinews asunder,

The bone-lockers bursted.   To Beowulf now
Was   the   battle-fame   given;   should   Grendel
    thenceforth   819
Flee life-sick awayward and under the fen-bents
Seek his unmerry stead : now wist he more surely
That ended his life was, and gone over for ever,
His day-tale told out.   But was for all Dane-folk
After that slaughter-race all their will done.
Then had he cleans'd for them, he the far-comer,
Wise and stout-hearted, the high hall of Hrothgar,
And sav'd it from war.   So the night-work he
    joy'd in
And his doughty deed done.   Yea, but he for the
    East-Danes
That lord of the Geat-folk his boast's end had
    gotten,
Withal their woes bygone all had he booted,   880
And the sorrow hate-fashion'd that afore they had
    dreed,
And the hard need and bitter that erst they must
    bear,
The sorrow unlittle.   Sithence was clear token
When the deer of the battle laid down there the
    hand
The arm and the shoulder, and all there together
Of the grip of that Grendel 'neath the great roof
    upbuilded.

XIV. THE DANES REJOICE; THEY GO TO LOOK ON THE SLOT OF GRENDEL, AND COME BACK TO HART, AND ON THE WAY MAKE MERRY WITH RACING AND THE TELLING OF TALES.

THERE was then on the morning, as I have
    heard tell it,
    Round the gift-hall a many of men of the
      warriors:
Were faring folk-leaders from far and from near
O'er the wide-away roads the wonder to look on,
The track of the loathly: his life-sundering
    nowise   841
Was deem'd for a sorrow to any of men there
Who gaz'd on the track of the gloryless wight;
How he all a-weary of mood thence awayward,
Brought to naught in the battle, to the mere of
    the nicors,
Now fey and forth-fleeing, his life-steps had flitted.
There all in the blood was the sea-brim a-welling,
The dread swing of the waves was washing all
    mingled
With hot blood; with the gore of the sword was
    it welling;
The death-doom'd had dyed it, sithence he un-
    merry   850

In his fen-hold had laid down the last of his life,
His soul of the heathen, and hell gat hold on him.
  Thence back again far'd they those fellows of old,
With many a young one, from their wayfaring
    merry,
Full proud from the mere-side on mares there
    a-riding
The warriors on white steeds.   There then was
    of Beowulf
Set forth the might mighty; oft quoth it a many
That nor northward nor southward beside the
    twin sea-floods,
Over all the huge earth's face now never another,
Never under the heaven's breadth, was there a
    better,   860
Nor of wielders of war-shields a worthier of king-
    ship;
But neither their friendly lord blam'd they one
    whit,
Hrothgar the glad, for good of kings was he.
There whiles the warriors far-famed let leap
Their fair fallow horses and fare into flyting
Where unto them the earth-ways for fair-fashion'd
    seemed,
Through their choiceness well kenned; and whiles
    a king's thane,
A warrior vaunt-laden, of lays grown bemindful,

E'en he who all many of tales of the old days
A multitude minded, found other words also   870
Sooth-bounden, and boldly the man thus began
E'en Beowulf's wayfare well wisely to stir,
With good speed to set forth the spells well areded
And to shift about words.   And well of all told he
That he of Sigemund erst had heard say,
Of the deeds of his might; and many things
        uncouth :
Of the strife of the Wælsing and his wide way-
        farings,
Of those that men's children not well yet they
        wist,
The feud and the crimes, save Fitela with him ;
Somewhat of such things yet would he say,   880
The eme to the nephew ; e'en as they aye were
In all strife soever fellows full needful ;
And full many had they of the kin of the eotens
Laid low with the sword.   And to Sigemund up-
        sprang
After his death-day fair doom unlittle
Sithence that the war-hard the Worm there had
        quelled,
The herd of the hoard ; he under the hoar stone,
The bairn of the Atheling, all alone dar'd it,
That wight deed of deeds ; with him Fitela was
        not.

But howe'er, his hap was that the sword so through-
    waded   890
The Worm the all-wondrous, that in the wall
    stood
The iron dear-wrought : and the drake died the
    murder.
There had the warrior so won by wightness,
That he of the ring-hoard the use might be
    having
All at his own will.   The sea-boat he loaded,
And into the ship's barm bore the bright fretwork
Wæls' son.   In the hotness the Worm was to-
    molten.
Now he of all wanderers was widely the greatest
Through the peoples of man-kind, the warder of
    warriors,   899
By mighty deeds ; erst then and early he throve.
Now sithence the warfare of Heremod waned,
His might and his valour, amidst of the eotens
To the wielding of foemen straight was he be-
    trayed,
And speedily sent forth : by the surges of sorrow
O'er-long was he lam'd, became he to his lieges,
To all of the athelings, a life-care thenceforward.
Withal oft bemoaned in times that were older
The ways of that stout heart many a carle of the
    wisest,

Who trow'd in him boldly for booting of bales,
And had look'd that the king's bairn should ever
    be thriving,   910
His father's own lordship should take, hold the
    folk,
The hoard and the ward-burg, and realm of the
    heroes,
The own land of the Scyldings.   To all men was
    Beowulf,
The Hygelac's kinsman to the kindred of men-
    folk,
More fair unto friends; but on Heremod crime
    fell.
  So whiles the men flyting the fallow street
    there
With their mares were they meting.   There then
    was the morn-light
Thrust forth and hasten'd; went many a warrior
All hardy of heart to the high hall aloft
The rare wonder to see; and the King's self
    withal   920
From the bride-bower wended, the warder of ring-
    hoards,
All glorious he trod and a mickle troop had he,
He for choice ways beknown; and his Queen
    therewithal
Meted the mead-path with a meyny of maidens.

XV. KING HROTHGAR AND HIS THANES LOOK ON THE ARM OF GRENDEL. CONVERSE BETWIXT HROTHGAR AND BEOWULF CONCERNING THE BATTLE.

OUT then spake Hrothgar; for he to the
    hall went,
  By the staple a-standing the steep roof he
    saw
Shining fair with the gold, and the hand there of
    Grendel :
  For this sight that I see to the All-wielder
    thanks
Befall now forthwith, for foul evil I bided,
All griefs from this Grendel; but God, glory's
    Herder,   930
Wonder on wonder ever can work.
Unyore was it then when I for myself
Might ween never more, wide all through my
    life-days,
Of the booting of woes; when all blood-be-
    sprinkled
The best of all houses stood sword-gory here;
Wide then had the woe thrust off each of the
    wise
Of them that were looking that never life-long

That land-work of the folk they might ward
    from the loathly,
From ill wights and devils.   But now hath a
    warrior
Through the might of the Lord a deed made
    thereunto   940
Which we, and all we together, in nowise
By wisdom might work.   What! well might be
    saying
That maid whosoever this son brought to birth
According to man's kind, if yet she be living,
That the Maker of old time to her was all-
    gracious
In the bearing of bairns.   O Beowulf, I now
Thee best of all men as a son unto me
Will love in my heart, and hold thou henceforward
Our kinship new-made now; nor to thee shall be
    lacking
As to longings of world-goods whereof I have
    wielding;   950
Full oft I for lesser things guerdon have given,
The worship of hoards, to a warrior was weaker,
A worser in strife.   Now thyself for thyself
By deeds hast thou fram'd it that liveth thy fair
    fame
For ever and ever.   So may the All-wielder
With good pay thee ever, as erst he hath done it.

Then Beowulf spake out, the Ecgtheow's bairn:
That work of much might with mickle of love
We framed with fighting, and frowardly ventur'd
The might of the uncouth; now I would that
    rather   960
Thou mightest have look'd on the very man
    there,
The foe in his fret-gear all worn unto falling.
There him in all haste with hard griping did I
On the slaughter-bed deem it to bind him indeed,
That he for my hand-grip should have to be lying
All busy for life: but his body fled off.
Him then I might not (since would not the
    Maker)
From his wayfaring sunder, nor naught so well
    sought I
The life-foe; o'er-mickle of might was he yet,
The foeman afoot: but his hand has he left us, 970
A life-ward, a-warding the ways of his wending,
His arm and his shoulder therewith. Yet in nowise
That wretch of the grooms any solace hath got
    him,
Nor longer will live the loathly deed-doer,
Beswinked with sins; for the sore hath him now
In the grip of need grievous, in strait hold to-
    gather'd
With bonds that be baleful: there shall he abide,

That wight dyed with all evil-deeds, the doom
    mickle,
For what wise to him the bright Maker will
    write it.   979
    Then a silenter man was the son there of Ecglaf
In the speech of the boasting of works of the battle,
After when every atheling by craft of the earl
Over the high roof had look'd on the hand there,
Yea, the fiend's fingers before his own eyen,
Each one of the nail-steads most like unto steel,
Hand-spur of the heathen one; yea, the own claw
Uncouth of the war-wight.   But each one there
    quoth it,
That no iron of the best, of the hardy of folk,
Would touch him at all, which e'er of the
    monster
The battle-hand bloody might bear away thence.

XVI. HROTHGAR GIVETH GIFTS TO BEOWULF.

THEN was speedily bidden that Hart be
    withinward   991
    By hand of man well adorn'd; was there a
    many
Of warriors and wives, who straightway that wine-
    house,

The guest-house, bedight them: there gold-shotten
    shone
The webs over the walls, many wonders to look on
For men every one who on such things will stare.
  Was that building the bright all broken about
All withinward, though fast in the bands of the
    iron;
Asunder the hinges rent, only the roof there
Was saved all sound, when the monster of evil 1000
The guilty of crime-deeds had gat him to flight
Never hoping for life.   Nay, lightly now may not
That matter be fled from, frame it whoso may
    frame it.
But by strife man shall win of the bearers of souls,
Of the children of men, compelled by need,
The abiders on earth, the place made all ready,
The stead where his body laid fast on his death-bed
Shall sleep after feast.   Now time and place was it
When unto the hall went that Healfdene's son,
And the King himself therein the feast should be
    sharing;   1010
Never heard I of men-folk in fellowship more
About their wealth-giver so well themselves
    bearing.
Then bow'd unto bench there the abounders in
    riches
And were fain of their fill.   Full fairly there took

A many of mead-cups the kin of those men,
The sturdy of heart in the hall high aloft,
Hrothgar and Hrothulf.   Hart there withinward
Of friends was fulfilled; naught there that was
    guilesome
The folk of the Scyldings for yet awhile framed.
  Gave then to Beowulf Healfdene's bairn   1020
A golden war-ensign, the victory's guerdon,
A staff-banner fair-dight, a helm and a byrny :
The great jewel-sword a many men saw them
Bear forth to the hero.   Then Beowulf took
The cup on the floor, and nowise of that fee-gift
Before the shaft-shooters the shame need he have.
Never heard I how friendlier four of the treasures,
All gear'd with the gold about, many men erewhile
On the ale-bench have given to others of men.
Round the roof of the helm, the burg of the head,
A wale wound with wires held ward from without-
    ward,   1031
So that the file-leavings might not over fiercely,
Were they never so shower-hard, scathe the shield-
    bold,
When he 'gainst the angry in anger should get him.
Therewith bade the earls' burg that eight of the
    horses
With cheek-plates adorned be led down the floor
In under the fences; on one thereof stood

A saddle all craft-bedeck'd, seemly with treasure.
That same was the war-seat of the high King full
    surely   1039
Whenas that the sword-play that Healfdene's son
Would work; never failed in front of the war
The wide-kenn'd one's war-might, whereas fell the
    slain.
  So to Beowulf thereon of either of both
The Ingwines' high warder gave wielding to have,
Both the war-steeds and weapons, and bade him
    well brook them.
Thuswise and so manly the mighty of princes,
Hoard-warden of heroes, the battle-race paid
With mares and with gems, so as no man shall
    blame them,
E'en he who will say sooth aright as it is.

XVII. THEY FEAST IN HART. THE GLEEMAN SINGS OF FINN AND HENGEST.

THEN the lord of the earl-folk to every
    and each one   1050
    Of them who with Beowulf the sea-ways
    had worn
Then and there on the mead-bench did handsel
    them treasure,

An heir-loom to wit; for him also he bade it
That a were-gild be paid, whom Grendel aforetime
By wickedness quell'd, as far more of them would
  he,
Save from them God all-witting the weird away
  wended,
And that man's mood withal. But the Maker
  all wielded
Of the kindred of mankind, as yet now he doeth.
Therefore through-witting will be the best every-
  where
And the forethought of mind. Many things must
  abide   1060
Of lief and of loth, he who here a long while
In these days of the strife with the world shall be
  dealing.
    There song was and sound all gather'd together
Of that Healfdene's warrior and wielder of battle,
The wood of glee greeted, the lay wreaked often,
Whenas the hall-game the minstrel of Hrothgar
All down by the mead-bench tale must be making:
    By Finn's sons aforetime, when the fear gat
      them,
The hero of Half-Danes, Hnæf of the Scyldings,
On the slaughter-field Frisian needs must he fall.
Forsooth never Hildeburh needed to hery   1071
The troth of the Eotens; she all unsinning

Was lorne of her lief ones in that play of the
    linden,
Her bairns and her brethren, by fate there they fell
Spear-wounded.   That was   the   all-woeful   of
    women.
Not unduly without cause the daughter of Hoc
Mourn'd the Maker's own shaping, sithence came
    the morn
When she under the heavens that tide came to see,
Murder-bale of her kinsmen, where most had she
    erewhile   1079
Of world's bliss.   The war-tide took all men away
Of Finn's thanes that were, save only a few ;
E'en so that he might not on the field of the
    meeting
Hold Hengest a war-tide, or fight any whit,
Nor yet snatch away thence by war the woe-
    leavings
From the thane of the King ; but terms now they
    bade him
That for them other stead all for all should make
    room,
A hall and high settle, whereof the half-wielding
They with the Eotens' bairns henceforth might
    hold,
And with fee-gifts moreover the son of Folkwalda
Each day of the days the Danes should beworthy ;

The war-heap of Hengest with rings should he
    honour   1091
Even so greatly with treasure of treasures,
Of gold all beplated, as he the kin Frisian
Down in the beer-hall duly should dight.
Troth then they struck there each of the two
    halves,
A peace-troth full fast. There Finn unto Hen-
    gest
Strongly, unstriveful, with oath-swearing swore,
That he the woe-leaving by the doom of the wise
    ones
Should hold in all honour, that never man hence-
    forth
With word or with work the troth should be
    breaking,   1100
Nor through craft of the guileful should undo it
    ever,
Though their ring-giver's bane they must follow
    in rank
All lordless, e'en so need is it to be:
But if any of Frisians by over-bold speaking
The murderful hatred should call unto mind,
Then naught but the edge of the sword should
    avenge it.
Then done was the oath there, and gold of the
    golden

Heav'd up from the hoard.   Of the bold Here-
    Scyldings
All yare on the bale was the best battle-warrior;
On the death-howe beholden was easily there 1110
The sark stain'd with war-sweat, the all-golden
    swine,
The iron-hard boar; there was many an atheling
With wounds all outworn; some on slaughter-
    field welter'd.
But Hildeburh therewith on Hnæf's bale she bade
    them
The own son of herself to set fast in the flame,
His bone-vats to burn up and lay on the bale there:
On his shoulder all woeful the woman lamented,
Sang songs of bewailing, as the warrior strode
    upward,
Wound up to the welkin that most of death-fires,
Before the howe howled; there molten the heads
    were,   1120
The wound-gates burst open, there blood was out-
    springing
From foe-bites of the body; the flame swallow'd
    all,
The greediest of ghosts, of them that war gat
    him
Of either of folks; shaken off was their life-
    breath.

XVIII. THE ENDING OF THE TALE OF FINN.

DEPARTED the warriors their wicks to visit
 All forlorn of their friends now, Friesland to look on,
Their homes and their high burg. Hengest a while yet
Through the slaughter-dyed winter bode dwelling with Finn
And all without strife : he remember'd his home-land,
Though never he might o'er the mere be a-driving   1130
The high prow be-ringed : with storm the holm welter'd,
Won war 'gainst the winds ; winter locked the waves
With bondage of ice, till again came another
Of years into the garth, as yet it is ever,
And the days which the season to watch never cease,
The glory-bright weather ; then gone was the winter,
And fair was the earth's barm. Now hasten'd the exile,

The guest from the garths; he on getting of
    vengeance
Of harms thought more greatly than of the sea's
    highway,
If he but a wrath-mote might yet be a-wending
Where the bairns of the Eotens might he still
    remember.   1141
The ways of the world forwent he in nowise
Then, whenas Hunlafing the light of the battle,
The best of all bills, did into his breast,
Whereof mid the Eotens were the edges well
    knowen.
Withal to the bold-hearted Finn befell after
Sword-bales the deadly at his very own dwell-
    ing,
When the grim grip of war Guthlaf and Oslaf
After the sea-fare lamented with sorrow
And wyted him deal of their woes; nor then
    might he   1150
In his breast hold his wavering heart. Was the
    hall dight
With the lives of slain foemen, and slain eke was
    Finn
The King 'midst of his court-men; and there
    the Queen, taken,
The shooters of the Scyldings ferry'd down to
    the sea-ships,

And the house-wares and chattels the earth-king
    had had,

E'en such as at Finn's home there might they
    find,

Of collars and cunning gems. They on the sea-
    path

The all-lordly wife to the Danes straightly
    wended,

Led her home to their people. So sung was the
    lay,

The song of the gleeman; then again arose
    game,   1160

The bench-voice wax'd brighter, gave forth the
    birlers

Wine of the wonder-vats. Then came forth
    Wealhtheow

Under gold ring a-going to where sat the two
    good ones,

The uncle and nephew, yet of kindred unsunder'd,

Each true to the other. Eke Unferth the spokes-
    man

Sat at feet of the Scyldings' lord ; each of his heart
    trow'd

That of mickle mood was he, though he to his
    kinsmen

Were un-upright in edge-play. Spake the dame
    of the Scyldings :

Now take thou this cup, my lord of the kingly,
Bestower of treasures! Be thou in thy joyance,
Thou gold-friend of men! and speak to these
    Geat-folk   1171
In mild words, as duly behoveth to do;
Be glad toward the Geat-folk, and mindful of
    gifts;
From anigh and from far peace hast thou as now.
To me one hath said it, that thou for a son
    wouldst
This warrior be holding. Lo! Hart now is
    cleansed,
The ring-hall bright-beaming. Have joy while
    thou mayest
In many a meed, and unto thy kinsmen
Leave folk and dominion, when forth thou must
    fare
To look on the Maker's own making. I know
    now   1180
My Hrothulf the gladsome, that he this young
    man
Will hold in all honour if thou now before him,
O friend of the Scyldings, shall fare from the
    world;
I ween that good-will yet this man will be yield-
    ing
To our offspring that after us be, if he mind him

Of all that which we two, for good-will and for
   worship,
Unto him erst a child yet have framed of kindness.
  Then along by the bench did she turn, where
    her boys were,
Hrethric and Hrothmund, and the bairns of high
   warriors,
The young ones together ; and there sat the good
   one,   1190
Beowulf the Geat, betwixt the two brethren.

XIX. MORE GIFTS ARE GIVEN TO BEOWULF. THE BRISING COLLAR TOLD OF.

BORNE to him then the cup was, and there-
   with friendly bidding
  In words was put forth ; and gold about
    wounden
All blithely they bade him bear ; arm-gearings
   twain,
Rail and rings, the most greatest of fashion of
   neck-rings
Of them that on earth I have ever heard tell of :
Not one under heaven wrought better was heard of
Midst the hoard-gems of heroes, since bore away
   Hama

To the bright burg and brave the neck-gear of
    the Brisings,
The gem and the gem-chest: from the foeman's
    guile fled he   1200
Of Eormenric then, and chose rede everlasting.
That ring Hygelac had, e'en he of the Geat-folk,
The grandson of Swerting, the last time of all
    times
When he under the war-sign his treasure defended,
The slaughter-prey warded. Him weird bore
    away
Sithence he for pride-sake the war-woe abided,
The feud with the Frisians; the fretwork he
    flitted,
The gem-stones much worthy, all over the waves'
    cup.
The King the full mighty cring'd under the shield;
Into grasp of the Franks the King's life was gotten
With the gear of the breast and the ring alto-
    gether;   1211
It was worser war-wolves then reft gear from the
    slain
After the war-shearing; there the Geats' war-folk
Held the house of the dead men. The Hall took
    the voices;
Spake out then Wealhtheow; before the host
    said she:

Brook thou this roundel, lief Beowulf, hence-
   forth,
Dear youth, with all hail, and this rail be thou
   using,
These gems of folk-treasures, and thrive thou
   well ever;
Thy might then make manifest! Be to these
   lads here
Kind of lore, and for that will I look to thy
   guerdon.   1220
Thou hast won by thy faring, that far and near
   henceforth,
Through wide time to come, men will give thee
   the worship,
As widely as ever the sea winds about
The windy land-walls. Be the while thou art
   living
An atheling wealthy, and well do I will thee
Of good of the treasures; be thou to my son
In deed ever friendly, and uphold thy joyance!
Lo! each of the earls here to the other is trusty,
And mild of his mood and to man-lord full
   faithful,
Kind friends all the thanes are, the folk ever
   yare.   1230
Ye well drunk of folk-grooms, now do ye my
   biddings.

To her settle then far'd she; was the feast of
    the choicest,
The men drank the wine nothing wotting of weird,
The grim shaping of old, e'en as forth it had gone
To a many of earls; sithence came the even,
And Hrothgar departed to his chamber on high,
The rich to his rest; and aright the house warded
Earls untold of number, as oft did they erewhile.
The bench-boards they bar'd them, and there
    they spread over
With beds and with bolsters.   Of the beer-
    skinkers one   1240
Who fain was and fey bow'd adown to his floor-
    rest.
At their heads then they rested their rounds of
    the battle,
Their board-woods bright-shining.   There on the
    bench was,
Over the atheling, easy to look on
The battle-steep war-helm, the byrny be-ringed,
The wood of the onset, all-glorious.   Their wont
    was
That oft and oft were they all yare for the war-tide,
Both at home and in hosting, were it one were it
    either,
And for every such tide as their liege lord unto
The need were befallen : right good was that folk.

XX. GRENDEL'S DAM BREAKS INTO HART AND BEARS OFF AESCHERE.

SO sank they to slumber; but one paid full
    sorely   1251
    For his rest of the even, as to them fell full
    often
Sithence that the gold-hall Grendel had guarded,
And won deed of unright, until that the end
    came
And death after sinning : but clear was it shown
    now,
Wide wotted of men, that e'en yet was a wreaker
Living after the loathly, a long while of time
After the battle-care, Grendel's own mother ;
The woman, the monster-wife, minded her woe,
She who needs must in horror of waters be won-
    ning,   1260
The streams all a-cold, sithence Cain was become
For an edge-bane forsooth to his very own brother,
The own son of his father.   Forth bann'd then
    he fared,
All marked by murder, from man's joy to flee,
And dwelt in the waste-land.   Thence woke there
    a many
Ghosts shapen of old time, of whom one was
    Grendel,

The fierce wolf, the hateful, who found him at
    Hart
A man there a-watching, abiding the war-tide;
Where to him the fell ogre to hand-grips befell;
Howe'er he him minded of the strength of his
    might,   1270
The great gift set fast in him given of God,
And trowed in grace by the All-wielder given,
His fostering, his staying; so the fiend he o'er-
    came
And bow'd down the Hell's ghost, that all humble
    he wended
Fordone of all mirth death's house to go look on,
That fiend of all mankind. But yet was his
    mother,
The greedy, the glum-moody, fain to be going
A sorrowful journey her son's death to wreak.
  So came she to Hart whereas now the Ring-
    Danes
Were sleeping adown the hall; soon there befell
Change of days to the earl-folk, when in she came
    thrusting,   1281
Grendel's mother: and soothly was minish'd the
    terror
By even so much as the craft-work of maidens,
The war - terror of wife, is beside the man
    weapon'd,

When the sword all hard bounden, by hammers
    to-beaten,
The sword all sweat-stain'd, through the swine
    o'er the war-helm
With edges full doughty down rightly sheareth.
    But therewith in the hall was tugg'd out the
    hard edge,
The sword o'er the settles, and wide shields a
    many
Heaved fast in the hand : no one the helm heeded,
Nor the byrny wide-wrought, when the wild fear
    fell on them.   1291
In haste was she then, and out would she thence-
    forth
For the saving her life, whenas she should be
    found there.
But one of the athelings she speedily handled
And caught up full fast, and fenward so fared.
But he was unto Hrothgar the liefest of heroes
Of the sort of the fellows ; betwixt the two sea-
    floods
A mighty shield-warrior, whom she at rest brake
    up,
A war-wight well famed.   There Beowulf was not ;
Another house soothly had erewhile been dighted
After gift of that treasure to that great one of
    Geats.   1301

Uprose cry then in Hart, all 'mid gore had she
    taken
The hand, the well-known, and now care wrought
    anew
In the wicks was arisen. Naught well was the
    bargain
That on both halves they needs must be buying
    that tide
With the life-days of friends. Then the lord
    king, the wise,
The hoary of war-folk, was harmed of mood
When his elder of thanes and he now unliving,
The dearest of all, he knew to be dead.
    To the bower full swiftly was Beowulf brought
    now,   1310
The man victory-dower'd; together with day-dawn
Went he, one of the earls, that champion be-
    worthy'd,
Himself with his fellows, where the wise was
    abiding
To wot if the All-wielder ever will to him
After the tale of woe happy change work.
Then went down the floor he the war-worthy
With the host of his hand, while high dinn'd the
    hall-wood,
Till he there the wise one with words had well
    greeted,

The lord of the Ingwines, and ask'd had the
    night been,
Since sore he was summon'd, a night of sweet
    easement.   1320

XXI. HROTHGAR LAMENTS THE SLAY-ING OF AESCHERE, AND TELLS OF GRENDEL'S MOTHER AND HER DEN.

SPAKE out then Hrothgar the helm of the
    Scyldings :
    Ask no more after bliss ; for new-made now
    is sorrow
For the folk of the Danes ; for Aeschere is
    dead,
He who was Yrmenlaf's elder of brethren,
My wise man of runes, my bearer of redes,
Mine own shoulder-fellow, when we in the war-
    tide
Warded our heads and the host on the host fell,
And the boars were a-crashing ; e'en such should
    an earl be,
An atheling exceeding good, e'en as was Aeschere.
Now in Hart hath befallen for a hand-bane unto
    him   1330
A slaughter-ghost wandering ; naught wot I
    whither

The fell one, the carrion-proud, far'd hath her
　　back-fare,
By her fill made all famous.　That feud hath she
　　wreaked
Wherein yesternight gone by Grendel thou
　　quelledst
Through thy hardihood fierce with grips hard
　　enow,
For that he over-long the lief people of me
Made to wane and undid.　In the war then he
　　cringed,
Being forfeit of life.　But now came another,
An ill-scather mighty, her son to awreak;
And further hath she now the feud set on foot,
As may well be deemed of many a thane,　　1341
Who after the wealth-giver weepeth in mind,
A hard bale of heart.　Now the hand lieth low
Which well-nigh for every joy once did avail you.
　　The dwellers in land here, my people indeed,
The wise-of-rede hall-folk, have I heard say e'en
　　this:
That they have set eyes on two such-like ere-
　　while,
Two mickle mark-striders the moorland a-holding,
Ghosts come from elsewhere, but of them one
　　there was,
As full certainly might they then know it to be,

In the likeness of woman; and the other shap'd
    loathly   1351
All after man's image trod the tracks of the exile,
Save that more was he shapen than any man other;
And in days gone away now they named him
    Grendel,
The dwellers in fold; they wot not if a father
Unto him was born ever in the days of erewhile
Of dark ghosts. They dwell in a dim hidden
    land,
The wolf-bents they bide in, on the nesses the
    windy,
The perilous fen-paths where the stream of the
    fell-side
Midst the mists of the nesses wends netherward
    ever,   1360
The flood under earth. Naught far away hence,
But a mile-mark forsooth, there standeth the
    mere,
And over it ever hang groves all berimed,
The wood fast by the roots over-helmeth the
    water.
But each night may one a dread wonder there see,
A fire in the flood. But none liveth so wise
Of the bairns of mankind, that the bottom may
    know.
Although the heath-stepper beswinked by hounds,

The hart strong of horns, that holt-wood should
    seek to   1369
Driven fleeing from far, he shall sooner leave life,
Leave life-breath on the bank, or ever will he
Therein hide his head.   No hallow'd stead is it:
Thence the blending of water-waves ever upriseth
Wan up to the welkin, whenso the wind stirreth
Weather-storms loathly, until the lift darkens
And weepeth the heavens.   Now along the rede
    wendeth
Of thee again only.   Of that earth yet thou
    know'st not,
The fearful of steads, wherein thou mayst find
That much-sinning wight; seek then if thou dare,
And thee for that feud will I guerdon with fee,
The treasures of old time, as erst did I do,   1381
With the gold all-bewounden, if away thence
    thou get thee.

XXII. THEY FOLLOW GRENDEL'S DAM TO HER LAIR.

SPAKE out then Beowulf the Ecgtheow's
    bairn :
    O wise of men, mourn not; for to each man
    'tis better
That his friend he awreak than weep overmuch.

Lo! each of us soothly abideth the ending
Of the life of the world.   Then let him work
    who work may
High deeds ere the death: to the doughty of
    war-lads
When he is unliving shall it best be hereafter.
Rise up, warder of kingdom! and swiftly now
    wend we   1390
The Grendel Kinswoman's late goings to look on;
And this I behote thee, that to holm shall she
    flee not,
Nor into earth's fathom, nor into the fell-holt,
Nor the grounds of the ocean, go whereas she
    will go.
For this one of days patience dree thou a while
    then
Of each one of thy woes, as I ween it of thee.
  Then leapt up the old man, and lightly gave
    God thank,
That mighty of Lords, for the word which the
    man spake.
And for Hrothgar straightway then was bitted a
    horse,
A wave-maned steed: and the wise of the
    princes   1400
Went stately his ways; and stepp'd out the man-
    troop,

F

The linden-board bearers. Now lightly the tracks
    were
All through the woodland ways wide to be seen
    there,
Her goings o'er ground ; she had gotten her
    forthright
Over the mirk-moor : bore she of kindred thanes
The best that there was, all bare of his soul,
Of them that with Hrothgar heeded the home.
Overwent then that bairn of the athelings
Steep bents of the stones, and stridings full narrow,
Strait paths nothing pass'd over, ways all uncouth,
Sheer nesses to wit, many houses of nicors.   1411
    He one of the few was going before
Of the wise of the men the meadow to look on,
Until suddenly there the trees of the mountains
Over the hoar-stone found he a-leaning,
A wood without gladness : the water stood under
Dreary and troubled. Unto all the Danes was it,
To the friends of the Scyldings, most grievous in
    mood
To many of thanes such a thing to be tholing,
Sore evil to each one of earls, for of Aeschere   1420
The head did they find e'en there on the holm-
    cliff;
The flood with gore welled (the folk looking on
    it),

With hot blood.   But whiles then the horn fell
    to singing
A song of war eager.   There sat down the band;
They saw down the water a many of worm-kind,
Sea-drakes seldom seen a-kenning the sound ;
Likewise on the ness-bents nicors a-lying,
Who oft on the undern-tide wont are to hold
    them
A course full of sorrow all over the sail-road.
Now the worms and the wild-deer away did they
    speed   1430
Bitter and wrath-swollen all as they heard it,
The war-horn a-wailing : but one the Geats'
    warden
With his bow of the shafts from his life-days
    there sunder'd,
From his strife of the waves ; so that stood in his
    life-parts
The hard arrow of war ; and he in the holm was
The slower in swimming as death away swept him.
So swiftly in sea-waves with boar-spears forsooth
Sharp-hook'd and hard-press'd was he thereupon,
Set on with fierce battle, and on to the ness tugg'd,
The wondrous wave-bearer ; and men were be-
    holding   1440
The grisly guest.   Beowulf therewith he gear'd
    him

With weed of the earls : nowise of life reck'd he:
Needs must his war-byrny, braided by hands,
Wide, many-colour'd by cunning, the sound seek,
E'en that which his bone-coffer knew how to ward,
So that the war-grip his heart ne'er a while,
The foe-snatch of the wrathful his life ne'er
    should scathe ;
Therewith the white war-helm warded his head,
E'en that which should mingle with ground of
    the mere,
And seek the sound-welter, with treasure be-
    worthy'd,   1450
All girt with the lordly chains, as in days gone by
The weapon-smith wrought it most wondrously
    done,
Beset with the swine-shapes, so that sithence
The brand or the battle-blades never might bite it.
Nor forsooth was that littlest of all of his main-
    stays,
Which to him in his need lent the spokesman of
    Hrothgar,
E'en the battle-sword hafted that had to name
    Hrunting,
That in fore days was one of the treasures of old,
The edges of iron with the poison twigs o'er-stain'd,
With battle-sweat harden'd ; in the brunt never
    fail'd he   1460

Any one of the warriors whose hand wound about
    him,
Who in grisly wayfarings durst ever to wend him
To the folk-stead of foemen.   Not the first of
    times was it
That battle-work doughty it had to be doing.
Forsooth naught remember'd that son there of
    Ecglaf,
The crafty in mighty deeds, what ere he quoth
All drunken with wine, when the weapon he lent
To a doughtier sword-wolf: himself naught he
    durst it
Under war of the waves there his life to adventure
And warrior-ship work.   So forwent he the glory,
The fair fame of valour.   Naught far'd so the
    other   1471
Syth he to the war-tide had gear'd him to wend.

XXIII. BEOWULF REACHETH THE MERE-BOTTOM IN A DAY'S WHILE, AND CONTENDS WITH GRENDEL'S DAM.

OUT then spake Beowulf, Ecgtheow's bairn :
    Forsooth be thou mindful, O great son of
      Healfdene,
O praise of the princes, now way-fain am I,

O gold-friend of men, what we twain spake afore-
time :
If to me for thy need it might so befall
That I cease from my life-days, thou shouldest be
ever
To me, forth away wended, in the stead of a
father.
Do thou then bear in hand these thanes of my
kindred,   1480
My hand-fellows, if so be battle shall have me ;
Those same treasures withal, which thou gavest
me erst,
O Hrothgar the lief, unto Hygelac send thou ;
By that gold then shall wot the lord of the Geat-
folk,
Shall Hrethel's son see, when he stares on the
treasure,
That I in fair man-deeds a good one have found me,
A ring-giver ; while I might, joy made I thereof.
And let thou then Unferth the ancient loom have,
The wave-sword adorned, that man kenned widely,
The blade of hard edges ; for I now with
Hrunting   1490
Will work me the glory, or else shall death get me.
   So after these words the Weder-Geats' chieftain
With might of heart hasten'd ; nor for answer
then would he

Aught tarry; the sea-welter straightway took
    hold on
The warrior of men : wore the while of a daytide
Or ever the ground-plain might he set eyes on.
    Soon did she find, she who the flood-ring
Sword-ravening had held for an hundred of seasons,
Greedy and grim, that there one man of grooms
The abode of the alien-wights sought from above ;
Then toward him she grasp'd and gat hold on the
    warrior   1501
With fell clutch, but no sooner she scathed within-
    ward
The hale body; rings from without-ward it warded,
That she could in no wise the war-skin clutch
    through,
The fast locked limb-sark, with fingers all loathly.
So bare then that sea-wolf when she came unto
    bottom
The king of the rings to the court-hall adown
In such wise that he might not, though hard-
    moody was he,
Be wielding of weapons. But a many of wonders
In sea-swimming swink'd him, and many a sea-deer
With his war-tusks was breaking his sark of the
    battle ;   1511
The fell wights him follow'd. 'Twas then the
    earl found it

That in foe-hall there was he, I wot not of which,
Where never the water might scathe him a whit,
Nor because of the roof-hall might reach to him
    there
The fear-grip of the flood. Now fire-light he saw,
The bleak beam forsooth all brightly a-shining.
Then the good one, he saw the wolf of the
    ground,
The mere-wife the mighty, and main onset made he
With his battle-bill; never his hand withheld
    sword-swing,   1520
So that there on her head sang the ring-sword for-
    sooth
The song of war greedy. But then found the guest
That the beam of the battle would bite not there-
    with,
Or scathe life at all, but there failed the edge
The king in his need.   It had ere thol'd a many
Of meetings of hand; oft it sheared the helm,
The host-rail of the fey one; and then was the
    first time
For that treasure dear lov'd that its might lay a-low.
But therewithal steadfast, naught sluggish of
    valour,
All mindful of high deeds was Hygelac's kinsman.
Cast then the wounden blade bound with the
    gem-stones   1531

The warrior all angry, that it lay on the earth
    there,
Stiff-wrought and steel-edged. In strength now
    he trusted,
The hard hand-grip of might and main; so shall
    a man do
When he in the war-tide yet looketh to winning
The praise that is longsome, nor aught for life
    careth.
Then fast by the shoulder, of the feud nothing
    recking,
The lord of the War-Geats clutch'd Grendel's
    mother,
Cast down the battle-hard, bollen with anger,
That foe of the life, till she bow'd to the floor ; 1540
But swiftly to him gave she back the hand-guerdon
With hand-graspings grim, and griped against
    him ;
Then mood-weary stumbled the strongest of
    warriors,
The foot-kemp, until that adown there he fell.
Then she sat on the hall-guest and tugg'd out
    her sax,
The broad and brown-edged, to wreak her her
    son,
Her offspring her own. But lay yet on his shoulder
The breast-net well braided, the berg of his life,

That 'gainst point and 'gainst edge the entrance
    withstood.
Gone amiss then forsooth had been Ecgtheow's
    son   1550
Underneath the wide ground there, the kemp of
    the Geats,
Save to him his war-byrny had fram'd him a help,
The hard host-net; and save that the Lord God
    the Holy
Had wielded the war-gain, the Lord the All-wise;
Save that the skies' Ruler had rightwisely doom'd it
All easily.   Sithence he stood up again.

XXIV. BEOWULF SLAYETH GRENDEL'S DAM, SMITETH OFF GRENDEL'S HEAD, AND COMETH BACK WITH HIS THANES TO HART.

MIDST the war-gear he saw then a bill
    victory-wealthy,
        An old sword of eotens full doughty of
    edges,
The worship of warriors.   That was choice of all
    weapons,   1559
Save that more was it made than any man other
In the battle-play ever might bear it afield,
So goodly, all glorious, the work of the giants.

Then the girdled hilt seiz'd he, the Wolf of the
    Scyldings,
The rough and the sword-grim, and drew forth
    the ring-sword,
Naught weening of life, and wrathful he smote
    then
So that there on her halse the hard edge begripped,
And brake through the bone-rings: the bill all
    through-waded
Her flesh-sheathing fey; cring'd she down on the
    floor;
The sword was war-sweaty, the man in his work
    joy'd.
The bright beam shone forth, the light stood
    withinward,   1570
E'en as down from the heavens' clear high aloft
    shineth
The sky's candle. He all along the house scanned;
Then turn'd by the wall along, heav'd up his
    weapon
Hard by the hilts the Hygelac's thane there,
Ireful one-reded; naught worthless the edge was
Unto the warrior; but rathely now would he
To Grendel make payment of many war-onsets,
Of them that he wrought on the folk of the West
    Danes
Oftener by mickle than one time alone,

Whenas he the hearthfellows of Hrothgar the
    King   1580
Slew in their slumber and fretted them sleeping,
Men fifteen to wit of the folk of the Danes,
And e'en such another deal ferry'd off outward,
Loathly prey. Now he paid him his guerdon
    therefor,
The fierce champion ; so well, that abed there he
    saw
Where Grendel war-weary was lying adown
Forlorn of his life, as him ere had scathed
The battle at Hart ; sprang wide the body,
Sithence after death he suffer'd the stroke,
The hard swing of sword. Then he smote the
    head off him.   1590
  Now soon were they seeing, those sage of the
    carles,
E'en they who with Hrothgar gaz'd down on the
    holm,
That the surge of the billows was blended about,
The sea stain'd with blood. Therewith the hoar-
    blended,
The old men, of the good one gat talking together
That they of the Atheling ween'd never eft-soon
That he, glad in his war-gain, should wend him
    a-seeking
The mighty king, since unto many it seemed

That him the mere-she-wolf had sunder'd and
   broken.
Came then nones of the day, and the ness there
   they gave up,   1600
The Scyldings the brisk; and then busk'd him
   home thence-ward
The gold-friend of men. But the guests, there
   they sat
All sick of their mood, and star'd on the mere;
They wist not, they ween'd not if him their own
   friend-lord
Himself they should see.
                 Now that sword began
Because of the war-sweat into icicles war-made,
The war-bill, to wane: that was one of the
   wonders
That it melted away most like unto ice
When the bond of the frost the Father lets loosen,
Unwindeth the wave-ropes, e'en he that hath
   wielding   1610
Of times and of seasons, who is the sooth Shaper.
  In those wicks there he took not, the Weder-
   Geats' champion,
Of treasure-wealth more, though he saw there a
   many,
Than the off-smitten head and the sword-hilts
   together

With treasure made shifting ; for the sword-blade
    was molten,
The sword broider'd was burn'd up, so hot was
    that blood,
So poisonous the alien ghost there that had died.
Now soon was a-swimming he who erst in the
    strife bode
The war-onset of wrath ones ; he div'd up through
    the water ;
And now were the wave-welters cleansed full well,
Yea the dwellings full wide, where the ghost of
    elsewhither   1621
Let go of his life-days and the waning of living.
    Came then unto land the helm of the ship-lads
Swimming stout-hearted, glad of his sea-spoil,
The burden so mighty of that which he bore there.
Yode then against him and gave thanks to God
That fair heap of thanes, and were fain of their
    lord,
For that hale and sound now they might see him
    with eyen ;
Then was from the bold one the helm and the
    byrny
All speedily loosen'd. The lake now was laid, 1630
The water 'neath welkin with war-gore bestained.
Forth then they far'd them alongst of the foot-
    tracks,

Men fain of heart all, as they meted the earth-
    way,
The street the well known ; then those king-bold
    of men
Away from the holm-cliff the head there they bore
Uneasily ever to each one that bore it,
The full stout-heart of men : it was four of them
    needs must
On the stake of the slaughter with strong toil
    there ferry
Unto the gold-hall the head of that Grendel ;
Until forthright in haste came into that hall, 1640
Fierce, keen in the hosting, a fourteen of men
Of the Geat-folk a-ganging ; and with them their
    lord,
The moody amidst of the throng, trod the mead-
    plains ;
Came then in a-wending the foreman of thanes,
The man keen of his deeds all beworshipp'd of
    doom,
The hero, the battle-deer, Hrothgar to greet.
Then was by the fell borne in onto the floor
Grendel's head, whereas men were a-drinking in
    hall,
Aweful before the earls, yea and the woman.
The sight wondrous to see the warriors there
    look'd on.   1650

XXV. CONVERSE OF HROTHGAR WITH BEOWULF.

SPAKE out then Beowulf, Ecgtheow's bairn :
What ! we the sea-spoils here to thee, son of
    Healfdene,
High lord of the Scyldings, with lust have brought
    hither
For a token of glory, e'en these thou beholdest.
Now I all unsoftly with life I escaped,
In war under the water dar'd I the work
Full hard to be worked, and well-nigh there was
The sundering of strife, save that me God had
    shielded.
So it is that in battle naught might I with
    Hrunting
One whit do the work, though the weapon be
    doughty ;   1660
But to me then he granted, the Wielder of men,
That on wall I beheld there all beauteous hanging
An ancient sword might-endow'd (often he leadeth
    right
The friendless of men) ; so forth drew I that
    weapon.
In that onset I slew there, as hap then appaid me,
The herd of the house ; then that bill of the
    host,

The broider'd sword, burn'd up, and that blood
    sprang forth
The hottest of battle-sweats; but the hilts thereof
    thenceforth
From the foemen I ferry'd.   I wreaked the foul
    deeds,
The death-quelling of Danes, e'en as duly behoved.
Now this I behote thee, that here in Hart mayst
    thou   1671
Sleep sorrowless henceforth with the host of thy men
And the thanes every one that are of thy people
Of doughty and young; that for them need thou
    dread not,
O high lord of Scyldings, on that behalf soothly
Life-bale for the earls as erst thou hast done.
    Then was the hilt golden to the ancient of
    warriors,
The hoary of host-leaders, into hand given,
The old work of giants; it turn'd to the owning,
After fall of the Devils, of the lord of the Danes,
That work of the wonder-smith, syth gave up the
    world   1681
The fierce-hearted groom, the foeman of God,
The murder-beguilted, and there eke his mother;
Unto the wielding of world-kings it turned,
The best that there be betwixt of the sea-floods
Of them that in Scaney dealt out the scat.

G

Now spake out Hrothgar, as he look'd on the
      hilts there,
The old heir-loom whereon was writ the be-
      ginning
Of the strife of the old time, whenas the flood
      slew,
The ocean a-gushing, that kin of the giants   1690
As fiercely they fared.   That was a folk alien
To the Lord everlasting; so to them a last guerdon
Through the welling of waters the Wielder did
      give.
So was on the sword-guards all of the sheer gold
By dint of the rune-staves rightly bemarked,
Set down and said for whom first was that sword
      wrought,
And the choice of all irons erst had been done,
Wreath-hilted and worm-adorn'd.   Then spake
      the wise one,
Healfdene's son, and all were gone silent:
    Lo that may he say, who the right and the
      soothfast   1700
Amid the folk frameth, and far back all remembers,
The old country's warden, that as for this earl
      here
Born better was he.   Uprear'd is the fame-blast
Through wide ways far yonder, O Beowulf, friend
      mine,

Of thee o'er all peoples.   Thou hold'st all with
    patience,
Thy might with mood-wisdom ; I shall make
    thee my love good,
As we twain at first spake it.   For a comfort thou
    shalt be
Granted long while and long unto thy people,
For a help unto heroes.   Naught such became
    Heremod
To Ecgwela's offspring, the honourful Scyldings ;
For their welfare naught wax'd he, but for felling
    in slaughter,   1711
For the quelling of death to the folk of the Danes.
Mood-swollen he brake there his board-fellows
    soothly,
His shoulder-friends, until he sunder'd him lonely,
That mighty of princes, from the mirth of all
    men-folk.
Though him God the mighty in the joyance of
    might,
In main strength, exalted high over all men,
And framed him forth, yet fast in his heart grew
A breast-hoard blood-fierce ; none of fair rings
    he gave
To the Danes as due doom would.   Unmerry
    he dured   1720
So that yet of that strife the trouble he suffer'd,

A folk-bale so longsome.   By such do thou learn
    thee,
Get thee hold of man-valour : this tale for thy
    teaching
Old in winters I tell thee.   'Tis wonder to say it,
How the high God almighty to the kindred of
    mankind
Through his mind the wide-fashion'd deals wis-
    dom about,
Home and earlship; he owneth the wielding of all.
At whiles unto love he letteth to turn
The mood-thought of a man that is mighty of
    kindred,
And in his land giveth him joyance of earth, 1730
And to have and to hold the high ward-burg of
    men,
And sets so 'neath his wielding the deals of the
    world,
Dominion wide reaching, that he himself may not
In all his unwisdom of the ending bethink him.
He wonneth well-faring, nothing him wasteth
Sickness nor eld, nor the foe-sorrow to him
Dark in mind waxeth, nor strife any where,
The edge-hate, appeareth ; but all the world for
    him
Wends as he willeth, and the worse naught he
    wotteth.

XXVI. MORE CONVERSE OF HROTH-GAR AND BEOWULF : THE GEATS MAKE THEM READY FOR DEPARTURE.

UNTIL that within him a deal of o'erthink-
  ing   1740
  Waxeth and groweth while sleepeth the
   warder,
The soul's herdsman; that slumber too fast is
  forsooth,
Fast bounden by troubles, the banesman all nigh,
E'en he that from arrow-bow evilly shooteth.
Then he in his heart under helm is besmitten
With a bitter shaft; not a whit then may he ward
  him
From the wry wonder-biddings of the ghost the
  all-wicked.
Too little he deems that which long he hath
  holden,
Wrath-greedy he covets; nor e'en for boast-sake
  gives
The rings fair beplated; and the forth-coming
  doom   1750
Forgetteth, forheedeth, for that God gave him
  erewhile,
The Wielder of glory, a deal of the worship.

At the ending-stave then it after befalleth
That the shell of his body sinks fleeting away,
And falleth all fey; and another one fetcheth,
E'en one that undolefully dealeth the treasure,
The earl's gains of aforetime, and fear never
    heedeth.
From the bale-envy ward thee, lief Beowulf,
    therefore,
Thou best of all men, and choose thee the better,
The redes everlasting; to o'erthinking turn not,
O mighty of champions! for now thy might
    breatheth   1761
For a short while of time; but eft-soon it shall be
That sickness or edges from thy strength thee
    shall sunder,
Or the hold of the fire, or the welling of floods,
Or the grip of the sword-blade, or flight of the
    spear,
Or eld the all-evil: or the beaming of eyen
Shall fail and shall dim: then shall it be forth-
    right
That thee, lordly man, the death over-masters.
E'en so I the Ring-Danes for an hundred of
    seasons
Did wield under the welkin and lock'd them by
    war   1770
From many a kindred the Middle-Garth over

With ash-spears and edges, in such wise that not
    ever
Under the sky's run of my foemen I reckon'd.
What! to me in my land came a shifting of that,
Came grief after game, sithence Grendel befell,
My foeman of old, mine ingoer soothly.
I from that onfall bore ever unceasing
Mickle mood-care ; herefor be thanks to the
    Maker,
To the Lord everlasting, that in life I abided,
Yea, that I on that head all sword-gory there,   1780
Now the old strife is over, with eyen should stare.
Go fare thou to settle, the feast-joyance dree thou,
O war-worshipp'd! unto us twain yet there
    will be
Mickle treasure in common when come is the
    morning.
  Glad of mood then the Geat was, and speedy
    he gat him
To go see the settle, as the sage one commanded.
Then was after as erst, that they of the might-
    fame,
The floor-sitters, fairly the feasting bedight them
All newly. The helm of the night loured over
Dark over the host-men. Uprose all the
    doughty,   1790
For he, the hoar-blended, would wend to his bed,

That old man of the Scyldings.   The Geat with-
    out measure,
The mighty shield-warrior, now willed him rest.
And soon now the hall-thane him of way-faring
    weary,
From far away come, forth show'd him the road,
E'en he who for courtesy cared for all things
Of the needs of the thane, e'en such as on that
    day
The farers o'er ocean would fainly have had.
  Rested then the wide-hearted; high up the
    house tower'd
Wide-gaping all gold-dight; within slept the
    guest;   1800
Until the black raven, the blithe-hearted, boded
The heavens' joy: then was come thither a-
    hastening
The bright sun o'er the plains, and hasten'd the
    scathers,
The athelings once more aback to their people
All fain to be faring; and far away thence
Would the comer high-hearted go visit his keel.
Bade then the hard one Hrunting to bear,
The Ecglaf's son bade to take him his sword,
The iron well-lov'd; gave him thanks for the
    lending,
Quoth he that the war-friend for worthy he told,

Full of craft in the war; nor with word blam'd
    he aught   1811
The edge of the sword. Hah! the high-hearted
    warrior.
So whenas all way-forward, yare in their war-gear,
Were the warriors, the dear one then went to the
    Danes,
To the high seat went the Atheling, whereas was
    the other;
The battle-bold warrior gave greeting to Hroth-
    gar.

XXVII. BEOWULF BIDS HROTHGAR FAREWELL: THE GEATS FARE TO SHIP.

OUT then spake Beowulf, Ecgtheow's bairn:
    As now we sea-farers have will to be say-
    ing,
We from afar come, that now are we fainest
Of seeking to Hygelac. Here well erst were we
Serv'd as our wills would, and well thine avail
    was.   1821
If I on the earth then, be it e'en but a little,
Of the love of thy mood may yet more be an-
    earning,
O lord of the men-folk, than heretofore might I,

Of the works of the battle yare then soon shall
    I be.
If I should be learning, I over the flood's run,
That the sitters about thee beset thee with dread,
Even thee hating as otherwhile did they;
Then thousands to theeward of thanes shall I
    bring
For the helping of heroes.   Of Hygelac wot I,
The lord of the Geat-folk, though he be but a
    youngling,   1831
That shepherd of folk, that me will he further
By words and by works, that well may I ward
    thee,
And unto thine helping the spear-holt may bear,
A main-staying mighty, whenas men thou art
    needing.
And if therewith Hrethric in the courts of the
    Geat-house,
The King's bairn, take hosting, then may he a
    many
Of friends find him soothly: far countries shall be
Better sought to by him who for himself is
    doughty.   1839
  Out then spake Hrothgar in answer to himward:
Thy word-saying soothly the Lord of all wisdom
Hath sent into thy mind; never heard I more
    sagely

In a life that so young was a man word be laying;
Strong of might and main art thou and sage of
    thy mood,
Wise the words of thy framing.   Tell I this for
    a weening,
If it so come to pass that the spear yet shall
    take,
Or the battle all sword-grim, the son of that
    Hrethel,
Or sickness or iron thine Alderman have,
Thy shepherd of folk, and thou fast to life hold
    thee,
Then no better than thee may the Sea-Geats be
    having   1850
To choose for themselves, no one of the kings,
Hoard-warden of heroes, if then thou wilt hold
Thy kinsman's own kingdom.   Me liketh thy
    mood-heart,
The longer the better, O Beowulf the lief;
In such wise hast thou fared, that unto the folks
    now,
The folk of the Geats and the Gar-Danes withal,
In common shall peace be, and strife rest appeased
And the hatreds the doleful which erst they have
    dreed;
Shall become, whiles I wield it, this wide realm
    of ours,

Treasures common to either folk: many a one
    other   1860
With good things shall greet o'er the bath of the
    gannet;
And the ring'd bark withal over sea shall be
    bringing
The gifts and love-tokens. The twain folks I
    know
Toward foeman toward friend fast-fashion'd to-
    gether,
In every way blameless as in the old wise.
   Then the refuge of warriors, he gave him withal,
Gave Healfdene's son of treasures yet twelve;
And he bade him with those gifts to go his own
    people
To seek in all soundness, and swiftly come back.
Then kissed the king, he of noble kin gotten, 1870
The lord of the Scyldings, that best of the thanes,
By the halse then he took him; from him fell
    the tears
From the blended of hoar hair. Of both things
    was there hoping
To the old, the old wise one; yet most of the
    other,
To wit, that they sithence each each might be
    seeing,
The high-heart in council. To him so lief was he

That he his breast-welling might nowise forbear,
But there in his bosom, bound fast in his heart-
  bonds,
After that dear man a longing dim-hidden
Burn'd against blood-tie. So Beowulf thence-
  forth,   1880
The gold-proud of warriors, trod the mould
  grassy,
Exulting in gold-store.   The sea-ganger bided
Its owning-lord whereas at anchor it rode.
Then was there in going the gift of King Hrothgar
Oft highly accounted ; yea, that was a king
In every wise blameless, till eld took from him
  eftsoon
The joyance of might, as it oft scathes a many.

XXVIII. BEOWULF COMES BACK TO HIS LAND. OF THE TALE OF THRYTHO.

CAME a many to flood then all mighty of
    mood,
  Of the bachelors were they, and ring-nets
    they bore,
The limb-sarks belocked.   The land-warden
  noted   1890
The earls' aback-faring, as erst he beheld them ;
Then nowise with harm from the nose of the cliff

The guests there he greeted, but rode unto them-
    ward,
And quoth that full welcome to the folk of the
    Weders
The bright-coated warriors were wending to ship.
Then was on the sand there the bark the wide-
    sided
With war-weed beladen, the ring-stemm'd as she
    lay there
With mares and with treasure; uptower'd the
    mast
High over Hrothgar's wealth of the hoards.
    He then to the boat-warden handsel'd a gold-
      bounden   1900
Sword, so that sithence was he on mead-bench
Worthy'd the more for that very same wealth,
The heirloom.   Sithence in the ship he departed
To stir the deep water; the Dane-land he left.
Then was by the mast there one of the sea-rails,
A sail, with rope made fast; thunder'd the sound-
    wood.
Not there the wave-floater did the wind o'er the
    billows
Waft off from its ways; the sea-wender fared,
Floated the foamy-neck'd forth o'er the waves,
The bounden-stemm'd over the streams of the
    sea ;   1910

Till the cliffs of the Geats there they gat them to
    wit,
The nesses well kenned. Throng'd up the keel
    then
Driven hard by the lift, and stood on the land.
Then speedy at holm was the hythe - warden
    yare,
E'en he who a long while after the lief men
Eager at stream's side far off had looked.
To the sand thereon bound he the wide-fathom'd
    ship
With anchor-bands fast, lest from them the waves'
    might
The wood that was winsome should drive thence
    awayward.
   Thereon bade he upbear the athelings' treasures,
The fretwork and wrought gold. Not far from
    them thenceforth   1921
To seek to the giver of treasures it was,
E'en Hygelac, Hrethel's son, where at home
    wonneth
Himself and his fellows hard by the sea-wall.
Brave was the builded house, bold king the lord
    was,
High were the walls, Hygd very young,
Wise and well-thriven, though few of winters
Under the burg-locks had she abided,

The daughter of Hæreth; naught was she das-
    tard;
Nowise niggard of gifts to the folk of the Geats,
Of wealth of the treasures.   But wrath Thrytho
    bore,   1931
The folk-queen the fierce, wrought the crime-deed
    full fearful.
No one there durst it, the bold one, to dare,
Of the comrades beloved, save only her lord,
That on her by day with eyen he stare,
But if to him death-bonds predestin'd he count on,
Hand-wreathed; thereafter all rathely it was
After the hand-grip the sword-blade appointed,
That the cunning-wrought sword should show
    forth the deed,
Make known the murder-bale.   Naught is such
    queenlike   1940
For a woman to handle, though peerless she be,
That a weaver of peace the life should waylay,
For a shame that was lying, of a lief man of men;
But the kinsman of Hemming, he hinder'd it
    surely.
    Yet the drinkers of ale otherwise said they;
That folk-bales, which were lesser, she framed
    forsooth,
Lesser enmity-malice, since thence erst she was
Given gold-deck'd to the young one of champions,

She the dear of her lineage, since Offa's floor
Over the fallow flood by the lore of her father 1950
She sought in her wayfaring.   Well was she
    sithence
There on the man-throne mighty with good ;
Her shaping of life well brooked she living ;
High love she held toward the lord of the heroes ;
Of all kindred of men by the hearsay of me
The best of all was he the twain seas beside,
Of the measureless kindred ; thereof Offa was
For gifts and for war, the spear-keen of men,
Full widely beworthy'd, with wisdom he held
The land of his heritage.   Thence awoke
    Eomær   1960
For a help unto heroes, the kinsman of Hemming,
The grandson of Garmund, the crafty in war-
    strife.

XXIX. BEOWULF TELLS HYGELAC OF HROTHGAR: ALSO OF FREAWARU HIS DAUGHTER.

WENT his ways then the hard one, and
            he with his hand-shoal,
        Himself over the sand the sea-plain a-
            treading,
The warths wide away ; shone the world's candle,

H

The sun slop'd from the southward; so dreed
    they their journey,
And went their ways stoutly unto where the earls'
    refuge,
The banesman of Ongentheow all in his burgs
    there,
The young king of war, the good, as they heard it,
Was dealing the rings. Aright unto Hygelac   1970
Was Beowulf's speeding made knowen full
    swiftly,
That there into the house-place that hedge of
    the warriors,
His mate of the linden-board, living was come,
Hale from the battle-play home to him house-
    ward.
Then rathe was beroomed, as the rich one was
    bidding,
For the guests a-foot going the floor all within-
    ward.
   Then sat in the face of him he from the fight
    sav'd,
Kinsman by kinsman, whenas his man-lord
In fair-sounding speech had greeted the faithful
With mightyful words. With mead-skinking
    turned   1980
Through the high house adown the daughter of
    Hæreth:

The people she loved : the wine-bucket bare she
To the hands of the men. But now fell to Hygelac
His very house-fellow in that hall the high
To question full fairly, for wit-lust to-brake him,
Of what like were the journeys the Sea-Geats had
    wended :
  How befell you the sea-lode, O Beowulf lief,
When thou on a sudden bethoughtst thee afar
Over the salt water the strife to be seeking,
The battle in Hart ? or for Hrothgar forsooth 1990
The wide-kenned woe some whit didst thou mend,
For that mighty of lords ? I therefore the mood-
    care
In woe-wellings seethed ; trow'd not in the
    wending
Of thee the lief man. A long while did I pray thee
That thou the death-guest there should greet not
    a whit ;
Wouldst let those same South-Danes their own
    selves to settle
The war-tide with Grendel. Now to God say I
    thank
That thee, and thee sound, now may I see.
  Out then spake Beowulf, Ecgtheow's bairn :
All undark it is, O Hygelac lord, 2000
That meeting the mighty, to a many of men ;

Of what like was the meeting of Grendel and me
On that field of the deed, where he many a deal
For the Victory-Scyldings of sorrow had framed,
And misery for ever ; but all that I awreaked,
So that needeth not boast any kinsman of Grendel
Any one upon earth of that uproar of dawn-dusk,
Nay not who lives longest of that kindred the
    loathly
Encompass'd of fenland.   Thither first did I come
Unto that ring-hall Hrothgar to greet ;   2010
Soon unto me the great Healfdene's son,
So soon as my heart he was wotting forsooth,
Right against his own son a settle there showed.
All that throng was in joy, nor life-long saw I
    ever
Under vault of the heavens amidst any hall-sitters
More mirth of the mead.   There the mighty
    Queen whiles,
Peace-sib of the folk, went all over the floor,
To the young sons bade heart up ; oft she there
    the ring-wreath
Gave unto a man ere to settle she wended.
At whiles fore the doughty the daughter of
    Hrothgar   2020
To the earls at the end the ale-bucket bore ;
E'en she whom Freawaru the floor-sitters thereat
Heard I to name ; where she the nail'd treasure

Gave to the warriors.   She was behight then
Youngling and gold-dight to the glad son of
    Froda.
This hath seemed fair to the friend of the
    Scyldings,
The herd of the realm, and good rede he ac-
    counts it,
That he with that wife of death-feuds a deal
And of strifes should allay.   Oft unseldom each-
    where
After a lord's fall e'en but for a little   2030
Bows down the bane-spear, though doughty the
    bride be.

XXX. BEOWULF FOREBODES ILL FROM THE WEDDING OF FREAWARU: HE TELLS OF GRENDEL AND HIS DAM.

ILL-LIKING this may be to the lord of the
    Heathobards,
    And to each of the thanes of that same people,
When he with fair bride on the floor of hall
    wendeth,
That the Dane's noble bairn his doughty should
    wait on,
As on him glisten there the heirlooms of the
    aged,

Hard and with rings bedight, Heathobards'
    treasure,
Whileas the weapons yet they might wield;
Till astray did they lead there at the lind-play
Their own fellows belov'd and their very own
    lives.   2040
For then saith at the beer, he who seeth the ring,
An ancient ash-warrior who mindeth of all
The spear-death of men; grim is he of mind;
Sad of mood he beginneth to tell the young
    champion,
Through the thought of his heart his mind there
    to try,
The war-bale to waken, and sayeth this word:
Mayest thou, friend mine, wot of the war-sword,
That which thy father bore in the fight
Under the war-mask e'en on the last time,
That the dear iron, whereas the Danes slew
    him,   2050
Wielded the death-field, since Withergyld lay,
After fall of the heroes, the keen-hearted
    Scyldings?
Now here of those banesmen the son, whoseso
    he be,
All merry in fretwork forth on floor fareth;
Of the murder he boasteth, and that jewel he
    beareth,

E'en that which of right thou shouldest arede.
Thus he mindeth and maketh word every of
    times,
With sore words he telleth, until the time cometh
That the thane of the fair bride for the deeds of
    his father
After bite of the bill sleepeth all blood-stain'd, 2060
All forfeit of life ; but thenceforth the other
Escapeth alive ; the land well he kenneth ;
Then will be broken on both sides forsooth
The oath-swearing of earls, whenas unto Ingeld
Well up the death-hatreds, and the wife-loves of him
Because of the care-wellings cooler become.
Therefore the Heathobards' faith I account not,
Their deal of the folk-peace, unguileful to Danes,
Their fast-bounden friendship. Henceforth must
    I speak on
Again about Grendel, that thou get well to
    know it,   2070
O treasure-out-dealer, how sithence betided
The hand-race of heroes : sithence heaven's gem
All over the grounds glided, came the wroth
    guest,
The dire night-angry one us to go look on,
Whereas we all sound were warding the hall.
There then for Handshoe was battle abiding,
Life-bale to the fey ; he first lay alow,

The war-champion girded; unto him became
    Grendel,
To the great thane of kindreds, a banesman of
    mouth,   2079
Of the man well-beloved the body he swallow'd;
Nor the sooner therefor out empty-handed
The bloody-tooth'd banesman, of bales all be-
    mindful,
Out from that gold-hall yet would he get him;
But he, mighty of main, made trial of me,
And gripp'd ready-handed. His glove hung aloft,
Wondrous and wide, in wily bands fast,
With cunning wiles was it begeared forsooth,
With crafts of the devils and fells of the dragons;
He me withinwards there, me the unsinning,
The doer of big deeds would do me to be   2090
As one of the many; but naught so it might be,
Sithence in mine anger upright I stood.
    'Tis over-long telling how I to the folk-
    scather
For each one of evils out paid the hand-gild.
There I, O my lord king, them thy leal people
Worthy'd with works: but away he gat loosed
Out thence for a little while, brooked yet life-
    joys;
But his right hand held ward of his track howso-
    ever,

High upon Hart-hall, and thence away humble
He sad of his mood to the mere-ground fell
 downward.   2100
 Me for that slaughter-race the friend of the
  Scyldings
With gold that beplated was mickle deal paid,
With a many of treasures, sithence came the
 morning,
And we to the feast-tide had sat us adown ;
Song was and glee there ; the elder of Scyldings,
Asking of many things, told of things o'erpast ;
Whiles hath the battle-deer there the harp's joy,
The wood of mirth greeted ; whiles the lay
 said he
Soothfast and sorrowful ; whiles a spell seldom
 told
Told he by right, the king roomy-hearted ; 2110
Whiles began afterward he by eld bounden,
The aged hoar warrior, of his youth to bewail
 him,
Its might of the battle ; his breast well'd within
 him,
When he, wont in winters, of many now minded.
 So we there withinward the livelong day's wear-
  ing
Took pleasure amongst us, till came upon men
Another of nights ; then eftsoons again

Was yare for the harm-wreak the mother of
    Grendel:
All sorry she wended, for her son death had taken,
The war-hate of the Weders: that monster of
    women   2120
Awreaked her bairn, and quelled a warrior
In manner all mighty. Then was there from
    Aeschere,
The wise man of old, life waning away;
Nor him might they even when come was the
    morning,
That death-weary wight, the folk of the Danes
Burn up with the brand, nor lade on the bale
The man well-belov'd, for his body she bare off
In her fathom the fiendly all under the fell-
    stream.
    That was unto Hrothgar of sorrows the heaviest
Of them which the folk-chieftain long had be-
    fallen.   2130
Then me did the lord king, and e'en by thy life,
Mood-heavy beseech me that I in the holm-
    throng
Should do after earlship, my life to adventure,
And frame me main-greatness, and meed he
    behight me.
Then I of the welling flood, which is well kenned,
The grim and the grisly ground-herder did find.

There to us for a while was the blending of hands;
The holm welled with gore, and the head I be-
     carved
In that hall of the ground from the Mother of
     Grendel
With the all-eked edges; unsoftly out thence 2140
My life forth I ferry'd, for not yet was I fey.
But the earls' burg to me was giving thereafter
Much sort of the treasures, e'en Healfdene's son.

XXXI. BEOWULF GIVES HROTHGAR'S GIFTS TO HYGELAC, AND BY HIM IS REWARDED. OF THE DEATH OF HYGELAC AND OF HEARDRED HIS SON, AND HOW BEOWULF IS KING OF THE GEATS: THE WORM IS FIRST TOLD OF.

SO therewith the folk-king far'd, living full
     seemly;
  By those wages forsooth ne'er a whit had I
     lost,
By the meed of my main, but to me treasure gave
     he,
The Healfdene's son, to the doom of myself;
Which to thee, king of bold ones, will I be
     a-bringing,

And gladly will give thee; for of thee is all
    gotten
Of favours along, and but little have I   2150
Of head-kinsmen forsooth, saving, Hygelac, thee.
  Then he bade them bear in the boar-shape, the
    head-sign,
The battle-steep war-helm, the byrny all hoary,
The sword stately-good, and spell after he said:
This raiment of war Hrothgar gave to my hand,
The wise of the kings, and therewithal bade me,
That I first of all of his favour should flit thee;
He quoth that first had it King Heorogar of old,
The king of the Scyldings, a long while of time;
But no sooner would he give it unto his son,   2160
Heoroward the well-whet, though kind to him
    were he,
This weed of the breast.   Do thou brook it full
    well.
  On these fretworks, so heard I, four horses
    therewith,
All alike, close followed after the track,
Steeds apple-fallow.   Fair grace he gave him
Of horses and treasures.   E'en thus shall do
    kinsman,
And nowise a wile-net shall weave for another
With craft of the darkness, or do unto death
His very hand-fellow.   But now unto Hygelac

The bold in the battle was his nephew full faith-
    ful,   2170
And either to other of good deeds was mindful.
I heard that the neck-ring to Hygd did he give,
E'en the wonder-gem well-wrought, that Wealh-
    theow gave him,
The king's daughter ; gave he three steeds there-
    withal
Slender, and saddle-bright ; sithence to her was,
After the ring-gift, the breast well beworthy'd.
   Thus boldly he bore him, the Ecgtheow's bairn,
The groom kenned in battle, in good deeds a-
    doing ;
After due doom he did, and ne'er slew he the
    drunken
Hearth-fellows of him : naught rough was his
    heart ;   2180
But of all men of mankind with the greatest of
    might
The gift fully and fast set, which had God to
    him given,
That war-deer did hold.   Long was he con-
    temned,
While the bairns of the Geats naught told him
    for good,
Nor him on the mead-bench worthy of mickle
The lord of the war-hosts would be a-making.

Weened they strongly that he were but slack then,
An atheling unkeen ; then came about change
To the fame-happy man for every foul harm.

Bade then the earls' burg in to be bringing, 2190
The king battle-famed, the leaving of Hrethel,
All geared with gold ; was not 'mid the Geats then
A treasure-gem better of them of the sword-kind,
That which then on Beowulf's barm there he laid;
And gave to him there seven thousand in gift,
A built house and king-stool ; to both them
     together
Was in that folkship land that was kindly,
Father-right, home ; to the other one rather
A wide realm, to him who was there the better.
But thereafter it went so in days later worn 2200
Through the din of the battle, sithence Hygelac
     lay low
And unto Heardred swords of the battle
Under the war-board were for a bane ;
When fell on him midst of this victory-folk
The hard battle-wolves, the Scyldings of war,
And by war overwhelmed the nephew of Hereric ;
That sithence unto Beowulf turned the broad
     realm
All into his hand.   Well then did he hold it
For a fifty of winters ; then was he an old king,
An old fatherland's warder ; until one began 2210

Through the dark of the night-tide, a drake, to
 hold sway,
In a howe high aloft watched over an hoard,
A stone-burg full steep; thereunder a path sty'd
Unknown unto men, and therewithin wended
Who of men do I know not; for his lust there
 took he,
From the hoard of the heathen his hand took away
A hall-bowl gem-flecked, nowise back did he
 give it
Though the herd of the hoard him sleeping be-
 guil'd he
With thief-craft; and this then found out the
 king,
The best of folk-heroes, that wrath-bollen
 was he.   2220

XXXII. HOW THE WORM CAME TO THE HOWE, AND HOW HE WAS ROBBED OF A CUP; AND HOW HE FELL ON THE FOLK.

NOT at all with self-wielding the craft of
 the worm-hoards
 He sought of his own will, who sore himself harmed;
But for threat of oppression a thrall, of I wot not

Which bairn of mankind, from blows wrathful
    fled,
House-needy forsooth, and hied him therein,
A man by guilt troubled.   Then soon it betided
That therein to the guest there stood grisly
    terror;
However the wretched, of every hope waning

   .   .   .   .

The ill-shapen wight, whenas the fear gat him,
The treasure-vat saw; of such there was a many
Up in that earth-house of treasures of old,   2231
As them in the yore-days, though what man I
    know not,
The huge leavings and loom of a kindred of high
    ones,
Well thinking of thoughts there had hidden away,
Dear treasures.   But all them had death borne
    away
In the times of erewhile; and the one at the last
Of the doughty of that folk that there longest
    lived,
There waxed he friend-sad, yet ween'd he to tarry,
That he for a little those treasures the longsome
Might brook for himself.   But a burg now all
    ready   2240
Wonn'd on the plain nigh the waves of the water,
New by a ness, by narrow-crafts fasten'd;

Within there then bare of the treasures of earls
That herd of the rings a deal hard to carry,
Of gold fair beplated, and few words he quoth:
 Hold thou, O earth, now, since heroes may
  hold not,
The owning of earls.   What! it erst within thee
Good men did get to them; now war-death hath
  gotten,
Life-bale the fearful, each man and every   2249
Of my folk; e'en of them who forwent the life:
The hall-joy had they seen.   No man to wear
  sword
I own, none to brighten the beaker beplated,
The dear drink-vat; the doughty have sought to
  else-whither.
Now shall the hard war-helm bedight with the
  gold
Be bereft of its plating; its polishers sleep,
They that the battle-mask erewhile should bur-
  nish:
Likewise the war-byrny, which abode in the battle
O'er break of the war-boards the bite of the irons,
Crumbles after the warrior; nor may the ring'd
  byrny
After the war-leader fare wide afield   2260
On behalf of the heroes: nor joy of the harp is,
No game of the glee-wood; no goodly hawk now

Through the hall swingeth; no more the swift
    horse
Beateth the burg-stead.   Now hath bale-quelling
A many of life-kin forth away sent.
    Suchwise sad-moody moaned in sorrow
One after all, unblithely bemoaning
By day and by night, till the welling of death
Touch'd at his heart.   The old twilight-scather
Found the hoard's joyance standing all open, 2270
E'en he that, burning, seeketh to burgs,
The evil drake, naked, that flieth a night-tide,
With fire encompass'd; of him the earth-dwellers
Are strongly adrad; wont is he to seek to
The hoard in the earth, where he the gold heathen
Winter-old wardeth; nor a whit him it betters.
    So then the folk-scather for three hundred
    winters
Held in the earth a one of hoard-houses
All-eked of craft, until him there anger'd
A man in his mood, who bare to his man-lord 2280
A beaker beplated, and bade him peace-warding
Of his lord: then was lightly the hoard searched
    over,
And the ring-hoard off borne; and the boon it
    was granted
To that wretched-wrought man.   There then the
    lord saw

That work of men foregone the first time of
    times.
Then awaken'd the Worm, and anew the strife
    was ;
Along the stone stank he, the stout-hearted found
The foot-track of the foe ; he had stept forth
    o'er-far
With dark craft, over-nigh to the head of the
    drake.
   So may the man unfey full easily outlive   2290
The woe and the wrack-journey, he whom the
    Wielder's
Own grace is holding. Now sought the hoard-
    warden
Eager over the ground ; for the groom he would
    find
Who unto him sleeping had wrought out the
    sore :
Hot and rough-moody oft he turn'd round the
    howe
All on the outward ; but never was any man
On the waste ; but however in war he rejoiced,
In battle-work. Whiles he turn'd back to his
    howe
And sought to his treasure-vat ; soon he found
    this,
That one of the grooms had proven the gold,   2300

The high treasures; then the hoard-warden abided,
But hardly forsooth, until come was the even,
And all anger-bollen was then the burg-warden,
And full much would the loath one with the fire-
    flame pay back
For his drink-vat the dear.   Then day was de-
    parted
E'en at will to the Worm, and within wall no
    longer
Would he bide, but awayward with burning he
    fared,
All dight with the fire: it was fearful beginning
To the folk in the land, and all swiftly it fell
On their giver of treasure full grievously ended.

XXXIII. THE WORM BURNS BEOWULF'S HOUSE, AND BEOWULF GETS READY TO GO AGAINST HIM.   BEOWULF'S EARLY DEEDS IN BATTLE WITH THE HETWARE TOLD OF.

BEGAN then the guest to spew forth of
    gleeds,   2311
    The bright dwellings to burn; stood the
    beam of the burning
For a mischief to menfolk; now nothing that
    quick was

The loathly lift-flier would leave there forsooth;
The war of the Worm was wide to be seen there,
The narrowing foe's hatred anigh and afar,
How he, the fight-scather, the folk of the Geats
Hated and harm'd; shot he back to the hoard,
His dark lordly hall, ere yet was the day's while;
The land-dwellers had he in the light low en-
    compass'd 2320
With bale and with brand; in his burg yet he
    trusted,
His war-might and his wall: but his weening
    bewray'd him.
  Then Beowulf was done to wit of the terror
Full swiftly forsooth, that the house of himself,
Best of buildings, was molten in wellings of fire,
The gift-stool of the Geats. To the good one
    was that
A grief unto heart; of mind-sorrows the greatest.
Weened the wise one, that Him, e'en the Wielder,
The Lord everlasting, against the old rights
He had bitterly anger'd; the breast boil'd within
    him 2330
With dark thoughts, that to him were naught
    duly wonted.
  Now had the fire-drake the own fastness of
    folk,
The water-land outward, that ward of the earth,

With gleeds to ground wasted; so therefore the
    war-king,
The lord of the Weder-folk, learned him ven-
    geance.
Then he bade be work'd for him, that fence of
    the warriors,
And that all of iron, the lord of the earls,
A war-board all glorious, for wissed he yarely
That the holt-wood hereto might help him no
    whit,
The linden 'gainst fire-flame.   Of fleeting days
    now   2340
The Atheling exceeding good end should abide,
The end of the world's life, and the Worm with
    him also,
Though long he had holden the weal of the hoard.
Forsooth scorned then the lord of the rings
That he that wide-flier with war-band should seek,
With a wide host; he fear'd not that war for
    himself,
Nor for himself the Worm's war accounted one
    whit,
His might and his valour, for that he erst a many
Strait-daring of battles had bided, and liv'd,
Clashings huge of the battle, sithence he of
    Hrothgar,   2350
He, the man victory-happy, had cleansed the hall,

And in war-tide had gripped the kindred of
    Grendel,
The loathly of kindreds ; nor was that the least
Of hand-meetings, wherein erst was Hygelac slain,
Sithence the Geats' king in the onrush of battle,
The lord-friend of the folks, down away in the
    Frieslands,
The offspring of Hrethel, died, drunken of sword-
    drinks,
All beaten of bill.   Thence Beowulf came forth
By his own craft forsooth, dreed the work of the
    swimming ;
He had on his arm, he all alone, thirty   2360
Of war-gears, when he to the holm went adown.
Then nowise the Hetware needed to joy them
Over the foot-war, wherein forth against him
They bore the war-linden : few went back again
From that wolf of the battle to wend to their
    homes.
  O'erswam then the waters' round Ecgtheow's
    son,
Came all wretched and byrd-alone back to his
    people,
Whereas offer'd him Hygd then the kingdom and
    hoard,
The rings and the king-stool : trowed naught in
    the child,

That he 'gainst folks outland the fatherland-
    seats   2370
Might can how to hold, now was Hygelac
    dead :
Yet no sooner therefor might the poor folk pre-
    vail
To gain from the Atheling in any of ways
That he unto Heardred would be for a lord,
Or eke that that kingdom henceforward should
    choose ;
Yet him midst of the folk with friend-lore he
    held,
All kindly with honour till older he waxed
And wielded the Weder-Geats. To him men-
    waifs thereafter
Sought from over the sea, the sons they or
    Ohthere,
For they erst had withstood the helm of the
    Scylfings,   2380
E'en him that was best of the kings of the sea,
Of them that in Swede-realm dealt out the
    treasure,
The mighty of princes. Unto him 'twas a life-
    mark ;
To him without food there was fated the life-
    wound,
That Hygelac's son, by the swinging of swords ;

And him back departed Ongentheow's bairn,
To go seek to his house, sithence Heardred lay
    dead,
And let Beowulf hold the high seat of the king
And wield there the Geats.   Yea, good was that
    king.

XXXIV. BEOWULF GOES AGAINST THE WORM.   HE TELLS OF HEREBEALD AND HÆTHCYN.

OF that fall of the folk-king he minded the
    payment   2390
    In days that came after: unto Eadgils he
    was
A friend to him wretched; with folk he upheld
    him
Over the wide sea, that same son of Ohthere,
With warriors and weapons.   Sithence had he
    wreaking
With cold journeys of care: from the king took
    he life.
  Now each one of hates thus had he outlived,
And of perilous slaughters, that Ecgtheow's son,
All works that be doughty, until that one day
When he with the Worm should wend him to
    deal.

So twelvesome he set forth all swollen with
    anger,   2400
The lord of the Geats, the drake to go look on.
Aright had he learnt then whence risen the feud
    was,
The bale-hate against men-folk : to his barm then
    had come
The treasure-vat famous by the hand of the finder ;
He was in that troop of men the thirteenth
Who the first of that battle had set upon foot,
The thrall, the sad-minded ; in shame must he
    thenceforth
Wise the way to the plain ; and against his will
    went he
Thereunto, where the earth-hall the one there he
    wist,   2409
The howe under earth anigh the holm's welling,
The wave-strife : there was it now full all within
With gems and with wires ; the monster, the
    warden,
The yare war-wolf, he held him therein the hoard
    golden,
The old under the earth : it was no easy cheaping
To go and to gain for any of grooms.
    Sat then on the ness there the strife-hardy
    king
While farewell he bade to his fellows of hearth,

The gold-friend of the Geats; sad was gotten his
    soul,
Wavering, death-minded; weird nigh beyond
    measure,
Which him old of years gotten now needs must
    be greeting,   2420
Must seek his soul's hoard and asunder must deal
His life from his body: no long while now was
The life of the Atheling in flesh all bewounden.
    Now spake out Beowulf, Ecgtheow's bairn:
Many a one in my youth of war-onsets I outliv'd,
And the whiles of the battle: all that I remember.
Seven winters had I when the wielder of treasures,
The lord-friend of folk, from my father me took,
Held me and had me Hrethel the king,
Gave me treasure and feast, and remember'd the
    friendship.   2430
For life thence I was not to him a whit loather,
A berne in his burgs than his bairns were, or each
    one,
Herebeald, or Hæthcyn, or Hygelac mine.
For the eldest there was in unseemly wise
By the mere deed of kinsman a murder-bed
    strawen,
Whenas him did Hæthcyn from out of his horn-
    bow,
His lord and his friend, with shaft lay alow:

His mark he miss'd shooting, and shot down his
    kinsman,
One brother another with shaft all bebloody'd;
That was fight feeless by fearful crime sinned, 2440
Soul-weary to heart, yet natheless then had
The atheling from life all unwreak'd to be
    ceasing.
So sad-like it is for a carle that is aged
To be biding the while that his boy shall be
    riding
Yet young on the gallows; then a lay should he
    utter,
A sorrowful song whenas hangeth his son
A gain unto ravens, and naught good of avail
May he, old and exceeding old, anywise frame.
Ever will he be minded on every each morning
Of his son's faring otherwhere; nothing he
    heedeth   2450
Of abiding another withinward his burgs,
An heritage-warder, then whenas the one
By the very death's need hath found out the ill.
Sorrow-careful he seeth within his son's bower
The waste wine-hall, the resting-place now of the
    winds,
All bereft of the revel; the riders are sleeping,
The heroes in grave, and no voice of the harp is,
No game in the garths such as erewhile was gotten.

XXXV. BEOWULF TELLS OF PAST FEUDS, AND BIDS FAREWELL TO HIS FELLOWS: HE FALLS ON THE WORM, AND THE BATTLE OF THEM BEGINS.

THEN to sleeping-stead wendeth he, singeth
   he sorrow,
  The one for the other; o'er-roomy all
   seem'd him   2460
The meads and the wick-stead. So the helm of
  the Weders
For Herebeald's sake the sorrow of heart
All welling yet bore, and in nowise might he
On the banesman of that life the feud be a-
  booting;
Nor ever the sooner that warrior might hate
With deeds loathly, though he to him nothing
  was lief.
  He then with the sorrow wherewith that sore
   beset him
Man's joy-tide gave up, and chose him God's
  light.
To his offspring he left, e'en as wealthy man
  doeth,
His land and his folk-burgs when he from life
  wended.   2470

Then sin was and striving of Swedes and of
    Geats,
Over the wide water war-tide in common,
The hard horde-hate to wit sithence Hrethel
    perish'd;
And to them ever were the Ongentheow's sons
Doughty and host-whetting, nowise then would
    friendship
Hold over the waters; but round about Hreosna-
    burgh
The fierce fray of foeman was oftentimes fram'd.
Kin of friends that mine were, there they awreaked
The feud and the evil deed, e'en as was famed;
Although he, the other, with his own life he
    bought it,   2480
A cheaping full hard: unto Hæthcyn it was,
To the lord of the Geat-folk, a life-fateful war.
Learned I that the morrow one brother the other
With the bills' edges wreaked the death on the
    banesman,
Whereas Ongentheow is a-seeking of Eofor:
Glode the war-helm asunder, the aged of Scylfings
Fell, sword-bleak; e'en so remember'd the hand
Feud enough; nor e'en then did the life-stroke
    withhold.
I to him for the treasure which erewhile he
    gave me

Repaid it in warring, as was to me granted,   2490
With my light-gleaming sword.   To me gave he land,
The hearth and the home-bliss : unto him was no need
That unto the Gifthas or unto the Spear-Danes
Or into the Swede-realm he needs must go seeking
A worse wolf of war for a worth to be cheaping ;
For in the host ever would I be before him
Alone in the fore-front, and so life-long shall I
Be a-framing of strife, whileas tholeth the sword,
Which early and late hath bestead me full often,
Sithence was I by doughtiness unto Day-raven   2500
The hand-bane erst waxen, to the champion of Hug-folk ;
He nowise the fretwork to the king of the Frisians,
The breast-worship to wit, might bring any more,
But cringed in battle that herd of the banner,
The Atheling in might : the edge naught was his bane,
But for him did the war-grip the heart-wellings of him
Break, the house of the bones.   Now shall the bill's edge,
The hand and hard sword, about the hoard battle.

So word uttered Beowulf, spake out the boast-
        word
For the last while as now : Many wars dared I 2510
In the days of my youth, and now will I yet,
The old warder of folk, seek to the feud,
Full gloriously frame, if the scather of foul-deed
From the hall of the earth me out shall be
        seeking.
    Greeted he then each one of the grooms,
The keen wearers of helms, for the last while of
        whiles,
His own fellows the dear : No sword would I
        fare with,
No weapon against the Worm, wist I but how
'Gainst the monster of evil in otherwise might I
Uphold me my boast, as erst did I with Grendel ;
But there fire of the war-tide full hot do I ween
        me,   2521
And the breath, and the venom ; I shall bear on
        me therefore
Both the board and the byrny ; nor the burg's
        warden shall I
Overflee for a foot's-breadth, but unto us twain
It shall be at the wall as to us twain Weird
        willeth,
The Maker of each man.   Of mood am I
        eager ;

So that 'gainst that war-flier from boast I with-
    hold me.
Abide ye upon burg with your byrnies bewarded,
Ye men in your battle-gear, which may the better
After the slaughter-race save us from wounding
Of the twain of us. Naught is it yours to take over,
Nor the measure of any man save alone me,   2532
That he on the monster should mete out his
    might,
Or work out the earlship: but I with my main
    might
Shall gain me the gold, or else gets me the battle,
The perilous life-bale, e'en me your own lord.
    Arose then by war-round the warrior renowned
Hard under helm, and the sword-sark he bare
Under the stone-cliffs: in the strength then he
    trowed
Of one man alone; no dastard's way such is.   2540
Then he saw by the wall (e'en he, who so many,
The good of man-bounties, of battles had out-liv'd,
Of crashes of battle whenas hosts were blended)
A stone-bow a-standing, and from out thence a
    stream
Breaking forth from the burg; was that burn's
    outwelling
All hot with the war-fire; and none nigh to the
    hoard then

K

Might ever unburning any while bide,
Live out through the deep for the flame of the
    drake.
  Out then from his breast, for as bollen as was he,
Let the Weder-Geats' chief the words be out
    faring;   2550
The stout-hearted storm'd and the stave of him
    enter'd
Battle-bright sounding in under the hoar stone.
Then uproused was hate, and the hoard-warden
    wotted
The speech of man's word, and no more while
    there was
Friendship to fetch.   Then forth came there first
The breath of the evil beast out from the stone,
The hot sweat of battle, and dinn'd then the
    earth.
  The warrior beneath the burg swung up his
    war-round
Against that grisly guest, the lord of the Geats;
Then the heart of the ring-bow'd grew eager
    therewith   2560
To seek to the strife.   His sword ere had he
    drawn,
That good lord of the battle, the leaving of old,
The undull of edges: there was unto either
Of the bale-minded ones the fear of the other.

All steadfast of mind stood against his steep
 shield
The lord of the friends, when the Worm was
 a-bowing
Together all swiftly, in war-gear he bided ;
Then boune was the burning one, bow'd in his
 going,
To the fate of him faring.   The shield was well
 warding
The life and the lyke of the mighty lord king   2570
For a lesser of whiles than his will would have
 had it,
If he at that frist on the first of the day
Was to wield him, as weird for him never will'd it,
The high-day of battle.   His hand he up braided,
The lord of the Geats, and the grisly-fleck'd
 smote he
With the leaving of Ing, in such wise that the
 edge fail'd,
The brown blade on the bone, and less mightily
 bit
Than the king of the nation had need in that
 stour,
With troubles beset.   But then the burg-warden
After the war-swing all wood of his mood   2580
Cast forth the slaughter-flame, sprung thereon
 widely

The battle-gleams : nowise of victory he boasted,
The gold-friend of the Geats; his war-bill had
      falter'd,
All naked in war, in such wise as it should not,
The iron exceeding good.   Naught was it easy
For him there, the mighty-great offspring of
      Ecgtheow,
That he now that earth-plain should give up for
      ever ;
But against his will needs must he dwell in the
      wick
Of the otherwhere country; as ever must each
      man
Let go of his loan-days.   Not long was it thence-
      forth   2590
Ere the fell ones of fight fell together again.
The hoard-warden up-hearten'd him, welled his
      breast
With breathing anew.   Then narrow need bore he,
Encompass'd with fire, who erst the folk wielded ;
Nowise in a heap his hand-fellows there,
The bairns of the athelings, stood all about him
In valour of battle ; but they to holt bow'd them ;
Their dear life they warded ; but in one of them
      welled   2598
His soul with all sorrow.   So sib-ship may never
Turn aside any whit to the one that well thinketh.

XXXVI. WIGLAF SON OF WEOHSTAN GOES TO THE HELP OF BEOWULF: NÆGLING, BEOWULF'S SWORD, IS BROKEN ON THE WORM.

WIGLAF so hight he, the son of Weohstan,
    Lief linden-warrior, and lord of Scyl-
      fings,
The kinsman of Aelfhere: and he saw his man-
    lord
Under his host-mask tholing the heat;
He had mind of the honour that to him gave he
    erewhile,
The wick-stead the wealthy of them, the Wæg-
    mundings,
And the folk-rights each one which his father
    had owned.
Then he might not withhold him, his hand gripp'd
    the round,
Yellow linden; he tugg'd out withal the old sword,
That was known among men for the heirloom of
    Eanmund,   2610
Ohthere's son, unto whom in the strife did be-
    come,
To the exile unfriended, Weohstan for the bane
With the sword-edge, and unto his kinsmen bare
    off

The helm the brown-brindled, the byrny beringed,
And the old eoten-sword that erst Onela gave
    him ;
Were they his kinsman's weed of the war,
Host-fight-gear all ready.   Of the feud nothing
    spake he,
Though he of his brother the bairn had o'er-
    thrown.
But the host-gear befretted he held many seasons,
The bill and the byrny, until his own boy might
Do him the earlship as did his ere-father.   2621
Amidst of the Geats then he gave him the war-
    weed
Of all kinds unnumber'd, whenas he from life
    wended
Old on the forth-way.   Then was the first time
For that champion the young that he the war-race
With his high lord the famed e'er he should
    frame :
Naught melted his mood, naught the loom of
    his kinsman
Weaken'd in war-tide ; that found out the Worm
When they two together had gotten to come.   2629
    Now spake out Wiglaf many words rightwise,
And said to his fellows : all sad was his soul :
I remember that while when we gat us the mead,
And whenas we behight to the high lord of us

In the beer-hall, e'en he who gave us these rings,
That we for the war-gear one while would pay,
If unto him thislike need e'er should befall,
For these helms and hard swords. So he chose
    us from host
To this faring of war by his very own will,
Of glories he minded us, and gave me these gems
    here,
Whereas us of gar-warriors he counted for good,
And bold bearers of helms. Though our lord
    e'en for us   2641
This work of all might was of mind all alone
Himself to be framing, the herd of the folk,
Whereas most of all men he hath mightiness
    framed,
Of deeds of all daring, yet now is the day come
Whereon to our man-lord behoveth the main
Of good battle-warriors; so thereunto wend we,
And help we the host-chief, whiles that the heat be,
The gleed-terror grim. Now of me wotteth God
That to me is much liefer that that, my lyke-
    body,   2650
With my giver of gold the gleed should engrip.
Unmeet it methinketh that we shields should bear
Back unto our own home, unless we may erst
The foe fell adown and the life-days defend
Of the king of the Weders. Well wot I hereof

That his old deserts naught such were, that he
    only
Of all doughty of Geats the grief should be bearing,
Sink at strife.   Unto us shall one sword be, one
    helm,
One byrny and shield, to both of us common.
    Through the slaughter-reek waded he then,
        bare his war-helm   2660
To the finding his lord, and few words he quoth:
    O Beowulf the dear, now do thee all well,
As thou in thy youthful life quothest of yore,
That naught wouldst thou let, while still thou
    wert living,
Thy glory fade out.   Now shalt thou of deeds
    famed,
The atheling of single heart, with all thy main
    deal
For the warding thy life, and to stay thee I will.
    Then after these words all wroth came the
    Worm,
The dire guest foesome, that second of whiles
With fire-wellings flecked, his foes to go look on,
The loath men.   With flame was lightly then
    burnt up   2671
The board to the boss, and might not the byrny
To the warrior the young frame any help yet.
But so the young man under shield of his kinsman

Went onward with valour, whenas his own was
All undone with gleeds ; then again the war-king
Remember'd his glories, and smote with main
    might
With his battle-bill, so that it stood in the head
Need-driven by war-hate.   Then asunder burst
    Nægling,
Waxed weak in the war-tide, e'en Beowulf's
    sword,   2680
The old and grey-marked ; to him was not given
That to him any whit might the edges of irons
Be helpful in battle ; over-strong was the hand
Which every of swords, by the hearsay of me,
With its swing over-wrought, when he bare unto
    strife
A wondrous hard weapon ; naught it was to him
    better.
  Then was the folk-scather for the third of
    times yet,
The fierce fire-drake, all mindful of feud ;
He rac'd on that strong one, when was room to
    him given,
Hot and battle-grim ; he all the halse of him
    gripped   2690
With bitter-keen bones ; all bebloody'd he waxed
With the gore of his soul.   Well'd in waves then
    the war-sweat.

XXXVII. THEY TWO SLAY THE WORM. BEOWULF IS WOUNDED DEADLY: HE BIDDETH WIGLAF BEAR OUT THE TREASURE.

THEN heard I that at need of the high
    king of folk
    The upright earl made well manifest might,
His craft and his keenness as kind was to him;
The head there he heeded not (but the hand
    burned
Of that man of high mood when he helped his
    kinsman),
Whereas he now the hate-guest smote yet a deal
    nether,
That warrior in war-gear, whereby the sword
    dived,
The plated, of fair hue, and thereby fell the flame
To minish thereafter, and once more the king's
    self   2701
Wielded his wit, and his slaying-sax drew out,
The bitter and battle-sharp, borne on his byrny;
Asunder the Weder's helm smote the Worm mid-
    most;
They felled the fiend, and force drave the life out,
And they twain together had gotten him ending,
Those athelings sib.   E'en such should a man be,

A thane good at need.   Now that to the king was
The last victory-while, by the deeds of himself,
Of his work of the world.   Sithence fell the
    wound,   2710
That the earth-drake to him had wrought but
    erewhile,
To swell and to sweal; and this soon he found
    out,
That down in the breast of him bale-evil welled,
The venom withinward; then the Atheling
    wended,
So that he by the wall, bethinking him wisdom,
Sat on seat there and saw on the works of the
    giants,
How that the stone-bows fast stood on pillars,
The earth-house everlasting upheld withinward.
    Then with his hand him the sword-gory,
That great king his thane, the good beyond
    measure,   2720
His friend-lord with water washed full well,
The sated of battle, and unspann'd his war-helm.
    Forth then spake Beowulf, and over his wound
    said,
His wound piteous deadly; wist he full well,
That now of his day-whiles all had he dreed,
Of the joy of the earth; all was shaken asunder
The tale of his days; death without measure nigh:

Unto my son now should I be giving
My gear of the battle, if to me it were granted
Any ward of the heritage after my days　　2730
To my body belonging.　This folk have I holden
Fifty winters; forsooth was never a folk-king
Of the sitters around, no one of them soothly,
Who me with the war-friends durst wend him to
　　greet,
And bear down with the terror.　In home have
　　I abided
The shapings of whiles, and held mine own well.
No wily hates sought I; for myself swore not many
Of oaths in unright.　For all this may I,
Sick with the life-wounds, soothly have joy.
Therefore naught need wyte me the Wielder of
　　men　　2740
With kin murder-bale, when breaketh asunder
My life from my lyke.　And now lightly go thou
To look on the hoard under the hoar stone,
Wiglaf mine lief, now that lieth the Worm
And sleepeth sore wounded, beshorn of his
　　treasure;
And be hasty that I now the wealth of old time,
The gold-having may look on, and yarely behold
The bright cunning gems, that the softlier may I
After the treasure-weal let go away
My life, and the folk-ship that long I have held.

XXXVIII. BEOWULF BEHOLDETH THE TREASURE AND PASSETH AWAY.

THEN heard I that swiftly the son of that
    Weohstan   2751
    After this word-say his lord the sore
    wounded,
Battle-sick, there obeyed, and bare forth his ring-
    net,
His battle-sark woven, in under the burg-roof;
Saw then victory-glad as by the seat went he,
The kindred-thane moody, sun-jewels a many,
Much glistering gold lying down on the ground,
Many wonders on wall, and the den of the Worm,
The old twilight-flier; there were flagons a-
    standing,   2759
The vats of men bygone, of brighteners bereft,
And maim'd of adornment; was many an helm
Rusty and old, and of arm-rings a many
Full cunningly twined. All lightly may treasure,
The gold in the ground, every one of mankind
Befool with o'erweening, hide it who will.
Likewise he saw standing a sign there all-golden
High over the hoard, the most of hand-wonders,
With limb-craft belocked, whence light a ray
    gleamed,
Whereby the den's ground-plain gat he to look on,

The fair works scan throughly. Not of the
    Worm there   2770
Was aught to be seen now, but the edge had un-
    done him.
Heard I then that in howe of the hoard was
    bereaving,
The old work of the giants, but one man alone,
Into his barm laded beakers and dishes
At his very own doom ; and the sign eke he took,
The brightest of beacons.   But the bill of the old
    lord
(The edge was of iron) erewhile it scathed
Him who of that treasure hand-bearer was
A long while, and fared a-bearing the flame-dread
Before the hoard hot, and welling of fierceness 2780
In the midnights, until that by murder he died.
    In haste was the messenger, eager of back-fare,
Further'd with fretted gems.   Him longing fordid
To wot whether the bold man he quick there shall
    meet
In that mead-stead, e'en he the king of the
    Weders,
All sick of his might, whereas he erst left him.
    He fetching the treasure then found the king
    mighty,
His own lord, yet there, and him ever all gory
At end of his life ; and he yet once again

Fell the water to warp o'er him, till the word's
    point   2790
Brake through the breast-hoard, and Beowulf
    spake out,
The aged, in grief as he gaz'd on the gold :
  Now I for these fretworks to the Lord of all
    thanking,
To the King of all glory, in words am yet saying,
To the Lord ever living, for that which I look on ;
Whereas such I might for the people of mine,
Ere ever my death-day, get me to own.
Now that for the treasure-hoard here have I sold
My life and laid down the same, frame still then
    ever
The folk-need, for here never longer I may be. 2800
So bid ye the war-mighty work me a howe
Bright after the bale-fire at the sea's nose,
Which for a remembrance to the people of me
Aloft shall uplift him at Whale-ness for ever,
That it the sea-goers sithence may hote
Beowulf's Howe, e'en they that the high-ships
Over the flood-mists drive from afar.
  Did off from his halse then a ring was all
    golden,
The king the great-hearted, and gave to his thane,
To the spear-warrior young his war-helm gold-
    brindled,   2810

The ring and the byrny, and bade him well brook
    them :
  Thou art the end-leaving of all of our kindred,
The Wægmundings ; Weird now hath swept all
    away
Of my kinsmen, and unto the doom of the Maker
The earls in their might ; now after them shall I.
  That was to the aged lord youngest of words
Of his breast-thoughts, ere ever he chose him the
    bale,
The hot battle-wellings ; from his heart now
    departed
His soul, to seek out the doom of the soothfast.

XXXIX. WIGLAF CASTETH SHAME ON THOSE FLEERS.

BUT gone was it then with the unaged
    man   2820
  Full hard that there he beheld on the earth
The liefest of friends at the ending of life,
Of bearing most piteous. And likewise lay his bane
The Earth-drake, the loathly fear, reft of his life,
By bale laid undone : the ring-hoards no longer
The Worm, the crook-bowed, ever might wield ;
For soothly the edges of the irons him bare off,
The hard battle-sharded leavings of hammers,

So that the wide-flier stilled with wounding
Fell onto earth anigh to his hoard-hall,   2830
Nor along the lift ever more playing he turned
At middle-nights, proud of the owning of treasure,
Show'd the face of him forth, but to earth there
      he fell
Because of the host-leader's work of the hand.
  This forsooth on the land hath thriven to few,
Of men might and main bearing, by hearsay of
      mine,
Though in each of all deeds full daring he were,
That against venom-scather's fell breathing he
      set on,
Or the hall of his rings with hand be a-stirring,
If so be that he waking the warder had found   2840
Abiding in burg.   By Beowulf was
His deal of the king-treasure paid for by death ;
There either had they fared on to the end
Of this loaned life.   Long it was not until
Those laggards of battle the holt were a-leaving,
Unwarlike troth-liars, the ten there together,
Who durst not e'en now with darts to be playing
E'en in their man-lord's most mickle need.
But shamefully now their shields were they
      bearing,
Their weed of the battle, there where lay the
      aged ;   2850

L

They gazed on Wiglaf where weary'd he sat,
The foot-champion, hard by his very lord's
shoulder,
And wak'd him with water: but no whit it sped
him;
Never might he on earth howsoe'er well he
will'd it
In that leader of spears hold the life any more,
Nor the will of the Wielder change ever a whit;
But still should God's doom of deeds rule the
rede
For each man of men, as yet ever it doth.
   Then from out of the youngling an answer
full grim   2859
Easy got was for him who had lost heart erewhile,
And word gave out Wiglaf, Weohstan's son,
The sorrowful-soul'd man: on those unlief he
saw:
Lo that may he say who sooth would be saying,
That the man-lord who dealt you the gift of those
dear things,
The gear of the war-host wherein there ye stand,
Whereas he on the ale-bench full oft was a-giving
Unto the hall-sitters war-helm and byrny,
The king to his thanes, e'en such as he choicest
Anywhere, far or near, ever might find: 2869
That he utterly wrongsome those weeds of the war

Had cast away, then when the war overtook him.
Surely never the folk-king of his fellows in battle
Had need to be boastful; howsoever God gave
    him,
The Victory-wielder, that he himself wreak'd him
Alone with the edge, when to him need of might
    was.
Unto him of life-warding but little might I
Give there in the war-tide; and yet I began
Above measure of my might my kinsman to help;
Ever worse was the Worm then when I with sword
Smote the life-foe, and ever the fire less strongly
Welled out from his wit.   Of warders o'er little
Throng'd about the king when him the battle
    befell.   2882
    Now shall taking of treasures and giving of
        swords
And all joy of your country-home fail from your
    kindred,
All hope wane away; of the land-right moreover
May each of the men of that kinsman's burg ever
Roam lacking; sithence that the athelings eft-
    soons
From afar shall have heard of your faring in
    flight,
Your gloryless deed.   Yea, death shall be better
For each of the earls than a life ever ill-fam'd. 2890

XL. WIGLAF SENDETH TIDING TO THE HOST: THE WORDS OF THE MESSENGER.

THEN he bade them that war-work give
    out at the barriers
    Up over the sea-cliff, whereas then the earl-
      host
The morning-long day sat sad of their mood,
The bearers of war-boards, in weening of both
    things,
Either the end-day, or else the back-coming
Of the lief man.   Forsooth he little was silent
Of the new-fallen tidings who over the ness rode,
But soothly he said over all there a-sitting:
   Now is the will-giver of the folk of the Weders,
The lord of the Geats, fast laid in the death-bed,
In the slaughter-rest wonneth he by the Worm's
    doings.   2901
And beside him yet lieth his very life-winner
All sick with the sax-wounds; with sword might
    he never
On the monster, the fell one, in any of manners
Work wounding at all.   There yet sitteth Wiglaf,
Weohstan's own boy, over Beowulf king,
One earl over the other, over him the unliving;
With heart-honours holdeth he head-ward withal

Over lief, over loath.   But to folk is a weening
Of war-tide as now, so soon as unhidden   2910
To Franks and to Frisians the fall of the king
Is become over widely.   Once was the strife shapen
Hard 'gainst the Hugs, sithence Hygelac came
Faring with float-host to Frisian land,
Whereas him the Hetware vanquish'd in war,
With might gat the gain, with o'er-mickle main;
The warrior bebyrny'd he needs must bow down:
He fell in the host, and no fretted war-gear
Gave that lord to the doughty, but to us was aye
     sithence
The mercy ungranted that was of the Merwing.
Nor do I from the Swede folk of peace or good
     faith   2921
Ween ever a whit.   For widely 'twas wotted
That Ongentheow erst had undone the life
Of Hæthcyn the Hrethel's son hard by the
     Raven-wood,
Then when in their pride the Scylfings of war
Erst gat them to seek to the folk of the Geats.
Unto him soon the old one, the father of Ohthere,
The ancient and fearful gave back the hand-stroke,
Brake up the sea-wise one, rescued his bride,
The aged his spouse erst, bereft of the gold,   2930
Mother of Onela, yea and of Ohthere ;
And follow'd up thereon his foemen the deadly,

Until they betook them and sorrowfully therewith
Unto the Raven-holt, reft of their lord.
With huge host then beset he the leaving of swords
All weary with wounds, and woe he behight them,
That lot of the wretched, the livelong night
    through;
Quoth he that the morrow's morn with the
    swords' edges
He would do them to death, hang some on the
    gallows   2939
For a game unto fowl.   But again befell comfort
To the sorry of mood with the morrow-day early;
Whereas they of Hygelac's war-horn and trumpet
The voice wotted, whenas the good king his ways
    came
Faring on in the track of his folk's doughty men.

XLI. MORE WORDS OF THE MESSENGER. HOW HE FEARS THE SWEDES WHEN THEY WOT OF BEOWULF DEAD.

WAS the track of the war-sweat of Swedes
    and of Geats,
    The men's slaughter-race, right wide to
    be seen,
How those folks amongst them were waking the
    feud.

Departed that good one, and went with his fellows,
Old and exceeding sad, fastness to seek ;
The earl Ongentheow upward returned ;   2950
Of Hygelac's battle-might oft had he heard,
The war-craft of the proud one ; in withstanding
    he trow'd not,
That he to the sea-folk in fight might debate,
Or against the sea-farers defend him his hoard,
His bairns and his bride.   He bow'd him aback
    thence,
The old under the earth-wall.   Then was the
    chase bidden
To the Swede-folk, and Hygelac's sign was up-
    reared,
And the plain of the peace forth on o'er-pass'd they,
After the Hrethlings onto the hedge throng'd.
There then was Ongentheow by the swords'
    edges,   2960
The blent-hair'd, the hoary one, driven to biding,
So that the folk-king fain must he take
Sole doom of Eofor.   Him in his wrath then
Wulf the Wonreding reach'd with his weapon,
So that from the stroke sprang the war-sweat in
    streams
Forth from under his hair ; yet naught fearsome
    was he,
The aged, the Scylfing, but paid aback rathely

With chaffer that worse was that war-crash of
    slaughter,
Sithence the folk-king turned him thither;
And nowise might the brisk one that son was of
    Wonred   2970
Unto the old carle give back the hand-slaying,
For that he on Wulf's head the helm erst had
    sheared,
So that all with the blood stained needs must he
    bow,
And fell on the field; but not yet was he fey,
But he warp'd himself up, though the wound
    had touch'd nigh.
But thereon the hard Hygelac's thane there,
Whenas down lay his brother, let the broad blade,
The old sword of eotens, that helm giant-fashion'd
Break over the board-wall, and down the king
    bowed,
The herd of the folk unto fair life was smitten.
There were many about there who bound up his
    kinsman,   2981
Upraised him swiftly when room there was made
    them,
That the slaughter-stead there at the stour they
    might wield,
That while when was reaving one warrior the
    other:

From Ongentheow took he the iron-wrought
    byrny,
The hard-hilted sword, with his helm all together :
The hoary one's harness to Hygelac bare he ;
The fret war-gear then took he, and fairly be-
    hight him
Before the folk due gifts, and even so did it ;
Gild he gave for that war-race, the lord of the
    Geats,   2990
The own son of Hrethel, when home was he
    come,
To Eofor and Wulf gave he over-much treasure,
To them either he gave an hundred of thousands,
Land and lock'd rings.   Of the gift none needed
    to wyte him
Of mid earth, since the glory they gained by
    battle.
Then to Eofor he gave his one only daughter,
An home-worship soothly, for pledge of his good
    will.
    That is the feud and the foeship full soothly,
The dead-hate of men, e'en as I have a weening,
Wherefor the Swede people against us shall
    seek,   3000
Sithence they have learned that lieth our lord
All lifeless ; e'en he that erewhile hath held
Against all the haters the hoard and the realm ;

Who after the heroes' fall held the fierce Scyl-
    fings,
Framed the folk-rede, and further thereto
Did earlship-deeds.   Now is haste best of all
That we now the folk-king should fare to be
    seeing,
And then that we bring him who gave us the
    rings
On his way to the bale : nor shall somewhat alone
With the moody be molten ; but manifold hoard
    is,   3010
Gold untold of by tale that grimly is cheapen'd,
And now at the last by this one's own life
Are rings bought, and all these the brand now
    shall fret,
The flame thatch them over : no earl shall bear off
One gem in remembrance ; nor any fair maiden
Shall have on her halse a ring-honour thereof,
But in grief of mood henceforth, bereaved of gold,
Shall oft, and not once alone, alien earth tread,
Now that the host-learn'd hath laid aside laughter,
The game and the glee-joy.   Therefore shall the
    spear,   3020
Full many a morn-cold, of hands be bewounden,
Uphoven in hand ; and no swough of the harp
Shall waken the warriors ; but the wan raven
    rather

Fain over the fey many tales shall tell forth,
And say to the erne how it sped him at eating,
While he with the wolf was a-spoiling the slain.
   So was the keen-whetted a-saying this while
Spells of speech loathly; he lied not much
Of weirds or of words.   Then uprose all the
    war-band,   3029
And unblithe they wended under the Ernes-ness,
All welling of tears, the wonder to look on.
Found they then on the sand, now lacking of soul,
Holding his bed, him that gave them the rings
In time erewhile gone by.   But then was the end-
    day
Gone for the good one; since the king of the
    battle,
The lord of the Weders, in wonder-death died.
But erst there they saw a more seldom-seen sight,
The Worm on the lea-land over against him
Down lying there loathly; there was the fire-
    drake,
The grim of the terrors, with gleeds all beswealed.
He was of fifty feet of his measure   3041
Long of his lying.   Lift-joyance held he
In the whiles of the night, but down again wended
To visit his den.   Now fast was he in death,
He had of the earth-dens the last end enjoyed.
There by him now stood the beakers and bowls,

There lay the dishes and dearly-wrought swords,
Rusty, through-eaten they, as in earth's bosom
A thousand of winters there they had wonned.
For that heritage there was, all craftily eked, 3050
Gold of the yore men, in wizardry wounden;
So that that ring-hall might none reach thereto,
Not any of mankind but if God his own self,
Sooth king of victories, gave unto whom he would
(He is holder of men) to open that hoard,
E'en to whichso of mankind should seem to him
    meet.

XLII. THEY GO TO LOOK ON THE FIELD OF DEED.

THEN it was to be seen that throve not the
    way
    To him that unrightly had hidden within
    there
The fair gear 'neath the wall. The warder erst
    slew
Some few of folk, and the feud then became 3060
Wrothfully wreaked. A wonder whenas
A valour-strong earl may reach on the ending
Of the fashion of life, when he longer in nowise
One man with his kinsmen may dwell in the
    mead-hall!

So to Beowulf was it when the burg's ward he
    sought,
For the hate of the weapons : he himself knew not
Wherethrough forsooth his world's sundering
    should be.
So until Doomsday they cursed it deeply,
Those princes the dread, who erst there had
    done it,
That that man should be of sins never sackless,
A-hoppled in shrines, in hell-bonds fast set, 3071
With plague-spots be punish'd, who that plain
    should plunder.
But naught gold-greedy was he, more gladly had
    he
The grace of the Owner erst gotten to see.
    Now spake out Wiglaf, that son was of Weoh-
    stan :
Oft shall many an earl for the will but of one
Dree the wrack, as to us even now is befallen :
Nowise might we learn the lief lord of us,
The herd of the realm, any of rede,
That he should not go greet that warder of
    gold,   3080
But let him live yet, whereas long he was lying,
And wonne in his wicks until the world's ending ;
But he held to high weird and the hoard hath
    been seen,

Grimly gotten: o'er hard forsooth was that
  giving,
That the king of the folk e'en thither enticed.
Lo! I was therein, and I look'd it all over,
The gear of the house, when for me room was
  gotten,
But I lightly in nowise had leave for the passage
In under the earth-wall; in haste I gat hold
Forsooth with my hands of a mickle main bur-
  den   3090
Of hoard-treasures, and hither then out did I
  bear them,
Out unto my king, and then quick was he yet,
Wise, and wit-holding: a many things spake he,
That aged in grief-care, and bade me to greet you,
And pray'd ye would do e'en after your friend's
  deeds
Aloft in the bale-stead a howe builded high,
Most mickle and mighty, as he amongst men was
The worthfullest warrior wide over the world,
While he the burg-weal erewhile might brook.
Then so let us hasten this second of whiles   3100
To see and to seek the throng of things strange,
The wonder 'neath wall; I shall wise you the way,
So that ye from a-near may look on enough
Of rings and broad gold; and be the bier swiftly
All yare thereunto, whenas out we shall fare.

Then let us so ferry the lord that was ours,
The lief man of men, to where long shall he
In the All-Wielder's keeping full patiently wait.
　　Bade then to bid the bairn of that Weohstan,
The deer of the battle, to a many of warriors,　3110
The house-owning wights, that the wood of the
　　bale
They should ferry from far, e'en the folk-owning
　　men,
Toward the good one.　And now shall the
　　gleed fret away,
The wan flame a-waxing, the strong one of
　　warriors,
Him who oft-times abided the shower of iron
When the storm of the shafts driven on by the
　　strings
Shook over the shield-wall, and the shaft held its
　　service,
And eager with feather-gear follow'd the barb.
　　Now then the wise one, that son was of Weoh-
　　stan,
Forth from the throng then call'd of the king's
　　thanes 　　　　　　　　　　　　　　　　3120
A seven together, the best to be gotten,
And himself went the eighth in under the foe-
　　roof;
One man of the battlers in hand there he bare

A gleam of the fire, of the first went he inward.
It was nowise allotted who that hoard should
    despoil,
Sithence without warden some deal that there
    was
The men now beheld in the hall there a-wonning,
Lying there fleeting; little mourn'd any,
That they in all haste outward should ferry
The dear treasures. But forthwith the drake
    did they shove,   3130
The Worm, o'er the cliff-wall, and let the wave
    take him,
The flood fathom about the fretted works' herd.
  There then was wounden gold on the wain
    laden
Untold of each kind, and the Atheling borne,
The hoary of warriors, out on to Whale-ness.

XLIII. OF THE BURIAL OF BEOWULF.

FOR him then they geared, the folk of the
    Geats,
    A pile on the earth all unweaklike that was,
With war-helms behung, and with boards of the
    battle,
And bright byrnies, e'en after the boon that he
    bade.

Laid down then amidmost their king mighty-
    famous   3140
The warriors lamenting, the lief lord of them.
Began on the burg of bale-fires the biggest
The warriors to waken : the wood-reek went up
Swart over the smoky glow, sound of the flame
Bewound with the weeping (the wind-blending
    stilled),
Until it at last the bone-house had broken
Hot at the heart.   All unglad of mind
With mood-care they mourned their own liege
    lord's quelling.
Likewise a sad lay the wife of aforetime
For Beowulf the king, with her hair all up-
    bounden,   3150
Sang sorrow-careful ; said oft and over
That harm-days for herself in hard wise she
    dreaded,
The slaughter-falls many, much fear of the
    warrior,
The shaming and bondage.   Heaven swallow'd
    the reek.
Wrought there and fashion'd the folk of the
    Weders
A howe on the lithe, that high was and broad,
Unto the wave-farers wide to be seen :
Then it they betimber'd in time of ten days,

M

The battle-strong's beacon; the brands' very
   leavings
They bewrought with a wall in the worthiest of
   ways,   3160
That men of all wisdom might find how to work.
   Into burg then they did the rings and bright
      sun-gems,
And all such adornments as in the hoard there
The war-minded men had taken e'en now;
The earls' treasures let they the earth to be hold-
   ing,
Gold in the grit, wherein yet it liveth,
As useless to men-folk as ever it erst was.
   Then round the howe rode the deer of the
      battle,
The bairns of the athelings, twelve were they in all.
Their care would they mourn, and bemoan them
   their king,   3170
The word-lay would they utter and over the man
   speak :
They accounted his earlship and mighty deeds
   done,
And doughtily deem'd them; as due as it is
That each one his friend-lord with words should
   belaud,
And love in his heart, whenas forth shall he
Away from the body be fleeting at last.

In such wise they grieved, the folk of the Geats,
For the fall of their lord, e'en they his hearth-
    fellows ;
Quoth they that he was a world-king forsooth,
The mildest of all men, unto men kindest,   3180
To his folk the most gentlest, most yearning of
    fame.

PERSONS AND PLACES

(Numbers refer to Pages)

BEANSTAN, father of Breca (31).

Beowulf the Dane (not Beowulf the Geat, the hero of the poem) was the grandfather of Hrothgar (2, 4).

Beowulf the Geat. *See* the Argument.

Breca (30), who contended with Beowulf in swimming, was a chief of the Brondings (31).

Brisings' neck-gear (70). "This necklace is the Brisingamen, the costly necklace of Freyja, which she won from the dwarfs and which was stolen from her by Loki, as is told in the Edda" (Kemble). In our poem, it is said that Hama carried off this necklace when he fled from Eormenric, king of the Ostrogoths.

DAYRAVEN (143), a brave warrior of the Hugs, and probably the slayer of Hygelac, whom, in that case, Beowulf avenged.

EADGILS, Eanmund (136, 137), "sons of Ohthere," and nephews of the Swedish King Onela, by whom they were banished from their native land for rebellion. They took refuge at the court of the Geat King Heardred, and Onela, "Ongentheow's bairn," enraged at their finding an asylum with his hereditary foes, invaded Geatland, and slew Heardred. At a later time Beowulf, when king of the

Geats, balanced the feud by supporting Eadgils in an invasion of Sweden, in which King Onela was slain.

Eanmund (149), while in exile at the court of the Geats, was slain by Weohstan, father of Wiglaf, and stripped of the armour given him by his uncle, the Swedish King Onela. Weohstan "spake not about the feud, although he had slain Onela's brother's son," probably because he was not proud of having slain an "exile unfriended" in a private quarrel.

Ecglaf, father of Unferth, Hrothgar's spokesman (29).

Ecgtheow (22), father of Beowulf the Geat, by the only daughter of Hrethel, king of the Geats. Having slain Heatholaf, a warrior of the Wylfings, Ecgtheow sought protection at the court of the Danish King Hrothgar, who accepted his fealty and settled the feud by a money-payment (27). Hence the heartiness of Beowulf's welcome at Hrothgar's hands.

Ecgwela. The Scyldings or Danes are once called " Ecgwela's offspring" (99). He may have been the founder of the older dynasty of Danish kings which ended with Heremod.

Eofor (142, 167–9), a Geat warrior, brother of Wulf. He came to the aid of his brother in his single combat with the Swedish King Ongentheow, and slew the king, being rewarded by Hygelac with the hand of his only daughter.

Eotens (61, 62, 66) are the people of Finn, king of Friesland. In other passages, it is merely a name for a race of monsters.

Finn (61–7). The somewhat obscure Finn episode in *Beowulf* appears to be part of a Finn epic, of which only the merest fragment, called the *Fight at Finnsburg*, is extant. The following conjectured outline of the whole

story is based on this fragment and on the Beowulf episode:
Finn, king of the Frisians, had carried off Hildeburh,
daughter of Hoc, probably with her consent. Her father,
Hoc, seems to have pursued the fugitives, and to have been
slain in the fight which ensued on his overtaking them.
After the lapse of some twenty years Hoc's sons, Hnæf
and Hengest, are old enough to undertake the duty of
avenging their father's death. They make an inroad into
Finn's country, and a battle takes place in which many
warriors, among them Hnæf and a son of Finn, are killed.
Peace is then solemnly concluded, and the slain warriors
are burnt. As the year is too far advanced for Hengest to
return home, he and those of his men who survive remain
for the winter in the Frisian country with Finn. But
Hengest's thoughts dwell constantly on the death of his
brother Hnæf, and he would gladly welcome any excuse
to break the peace which had been sworn by both parties.
His ill-concealed desire for revenge is noticed by the
Frisians, who anticipate it by themselves attacking Hengest
and his men whilst they are sleeping in the hall. This
is the night attack described in the *Fight at Finnsburg*.
It would seem that after a brave and desperate resistance
Hengest himself falls in this fight at the hands of the son
of Hunlaf (66), but two of his retainers, Guthlaf and
Oslaf, succeed in cutting their way through their enemies
and in escaping to their own land. They return with
fresh troops, attack and slay Finn, and carry his queen
Hildeburh back to the Daneland.

Folkwalda (62), father of Finn.

Franks (70, 165). Hygelac, king of the Geats, was defeated and slain early in the sixth century, in his historical
invasion of the Netherlands, by a combined army of Frisians,
Franks, and Hugs.

Freawaru (116), daughter of Hrothgar and Wealhtheow. Beowulf tells Hygelac that her father has betrothed her to Ingeld, prince of the Heathobards, in the hope of settling the feud between the two peoples. But he prophesies that the hope will prove vain : for an old Heathobard warrior, seeing a Danish chieftain accompany Freawaru to their court laden with Heathobard spoils, will incite the son of the former owner of the plundered treasure to revenge, until blood is shed, and the feud is renewed. That this was what afterwards befell, we learn from the Old English poem *Widsith*. *See also* ll. 83–5.

Friesland (65), the land of the North Frisians.

Frieslands (135), Frisian land (165), the home of the West Frisians.

Frisians. Two tribes are to be distinguished : 1. The North Frisians (61, 63), the people of Finn. 2. The West Frisians (143, 165), who combined with the Franks and Hugs and defeated Hygelac, between 512 and 520 A.D.

Froda (117), father of Ingeld. *See* Freawaru.

GUTHLAF and Oslaf (66). *See* Finn.

HÆRETH (112, 114), father of Hygd, wife of Hygelac.

Hæthcyn (139, 142, 165), second son of Hrethel, king of the Geats, and thus elder brother of Hygelac. He accidentally killed his elder brother Herebeald with a bow-shot, to the inconsolable grief of Hrethel. He succeeded to the throne at his father's death, but fell in battle at Ravenwood (165) by the hand of the Swedish King Ongentheow.

Half-Danes (61), the tribe to which Hnæf belongs. *See* Finn.

Hama (69). *See* Brisings.

Healfdene (4), king of the Danes, son of Beowulf the Scylding, and father of Hrothgar, "Healfdene's son" (16).

Heardred (126, 136-7), son of Hygelac and Hygd. While
still under age he succeeds his father as king of the Geats,
Beowulf, who has refused the throne himself, being his
counsellor and protector. He is slain by "Ongentheow's
bairn" (137), Onela, king of the Swedes.

Heathobards, Lombards, the tribe of Ingeld, the betrothed of
Freawaru, Hrothgar's daughter (117).

Heatholaf (27). *See* Ecgtheow.

Helmings. "The Dame of the Helmings" (36) is Hrothgar's
queen, Wealhtheow.

Hemming. "The Kinsman of Hemming" is a name for Offa
(112) and for his son Eomær (113).

Hengest (62-5). *See* Finn.

Heorogar (5), elder brother of Hrothgar (27), did not leave
his armour to his son Heoroward (124); but Hrothgar
gives it to Beowulf, and Beowulf gives it to Hygelac.

Herebeald (139, 141), eldest son of the Geat King Hrethel,
was accidentally shot dead with an arrow by his brother
Hæthcyn.

Heremod (53, 99) is twice spoken of as a bad and cruel Danish
king. In the end he is betrayed into the hands of his foes.

Hereric may have been brother of Hygd, Hygelac's queen, for
their son Heardred is spoken of as "the nephew of
Hereric" (126).

Here-Scyldings (64), Army-Scyldings, a name of the Danes.

Hetware (135, 165), the Hattuarii of the *Historia Francorum*
of Gregory of Tours and of the *Gesta Regum Francorum*, were the tribe against which Hygelac was raiding
when he was defeated and slain by an army of Frisians,
Franks, and Hugs.

Hildeburh (61, 64). *See* Finn.

Hnæf (61, 64). *See* Finn.

Hoc (62). *See* Finn.

Hrethel, a former king of the Geats; son of Swerting (70), father of Hygelac and grandfather of Beowulf (22), to whom he left his coat of mail (26). He died of grief at the loss of his eldest son Herebeald (139–41), who was accidentally slain by his brother Hæthcyn.

Hrethlings (167), the people of Hrethel, the Geats.

Hrethmen (26), Triumph-men, the Danes.

Hrethric (69, 106), elder son of Hrothgar and Wealhtheow.

Hrothgar. *See* the Argument.

Hrothulf (59, 68), probably the son of Hrothgar's younger brother Halga (5). He lives at the Danish court. Wealhtheow hopes that, if he survives Hrothgar, he will be good to their children in return for their kindness to him. It would seem that this hope was not to be fulfilled ("yet of kindred unsunder'd," 67).

Hygd, daughter of Hæreth, wife of Hygelac, the king of the Geats, and mother of Heardred. She may well be "the wife of aforetime" (177).

Hygelac, third son of Hrethel (139) and uncle to Beowulf, is the reigning king of the Geats during the greater part of the action of the poem. When his brother Hæthcyn was defeated and slain by Ongentheow at Ravenwood (165), Hygelac quickly went in pursuit and put Ongentheow to flight; but although, as leader of the attack, he is called "the banesman of Ongentheow" (114), the actual slayer was Eofor (142, 167), whom Hygelac rewarded with the hand of his only daughter (169). Hygelac came by his death between 512 and 520 A.D., in his historical invasion of the Netherlands, which is referred to in the poem four times (70, 135, 143, 165).

Ing (147). *See* Ingwines.

Ingeld (119). *See* Freawaru.

Ingwines (60, 77), "friends of Ing," the Danes. Ing, according to the Old English *Rune-Poem*, "was first seen by men amid the East Danes"; he has been identified with Frea.

MERWING, The (165), the Merovingian king of the Franks.

OFFA (113). *See* Thrytho.

Ohthere (136–7, 165), son of the Swedish King Ongentheow, and father of Eanmund and Eadgils (*q.v.*).

Onela, "Ongentheow's bairn" (137) and elder brother of Ohthere, is king of Sweden ("the helm of the Scylfings," 136) at the time of the rebellion of Eanmund and Eadgils. He invades the land of the Geats, which has harboured the rebels, slays Heardred, son of Hygelac, and then retreats before Beowulf. At a later time Beowulf avenges the death of Heardred by supporting Eadgils, "son of Ohthere" (137), in an invasion of Sweden, in which Onela is slain. *See also* Eadgils; and compare the slaying of Ali by Athils on the ice of Lake Wener in the Icelandic "Heimskringla."

Ongentheow, father of Onela and Ohthere, was a former king of the Swedes. The earlier strife between the Swedes and the Geats, in which he is the chief figure, is fully related by the messenger (164) who brings the tidings of Beowulf's death. In retaliation for the marauding invasions of Onela and Ohthere (142), Hæthcyn invaded Sweden, and took Ongentheow's queen prisoner. Ongentheow in return invaded the land of her captor, whom he slew, and rescued his wife (165); but in his hour of triumph he was attacked in his turn by Hygelac near Ravenwood, and fell by the hand of Eofor (168).

Scaney (97), Scede-lands (2), the most southern portion of the Scandinavian peninsula, belonging to the Danes; used in our poem for the whole Danish kingdom.

Scyld (1), son of Sheaf, was the mythical founder of the royal Danish dynasty of Scyldings.

Scyldings, descendants of Scyld, properly the name of the reigning Danish dynasty, is commonly extended to include the Danish people (3).

Scylfing: "the Scylfing" (167), "the aged of Scylfings" (142), is Ongentheow.

Scylfings (136), the name of the reigning Swedish dynasty, was extended to the Swedish people in the same way as "Scyldings" to the Danes. Beowulf's kinsman Wiglaf is called "lord of Scylfings" (149), and in another passage the name is apparently applied to the Geats (170); this seems to point to a common ancestry of Swedes and Geats, or it may be that Beowulf's father Ecgtheow was a "Scylfing."

Thrytho (112), wife of the Angle King Offa and mother of Eomær, is mentioned in contrast to Hygd, just as Heremod is a foil to Beowulf. She is at first the type of a cruel, unwomanly queen. But by her marriage with Offa, who seems to be her second husband, she is subdued and changed until her fame even adds glory to his.

Unferth, son of Ecglaf, is the spokesman of Hrothgar, at whose feet he sits. He is of a jealous disposition, and is twice spoken of as the murderer of his own brothers (34, 67). Taunting Beowulf with defeat in his swimming-match with Breca, he is silenced by the hero's reply, and more effectually still by the issue of the struggle with Grendel (57). Afterwards, however, he lends his sword Hrunting for Beowulf's encounter with Grendel's mother (85, 104).

WÆGMUNDINGS (149, 160), the family to which both Beowulf and Wiglaf belong. Their fathers, Ecgtheow and Weohstan, may have been sons of Wægmund.

Wedermark (17), the land of the Weder-Geats, *i.e.* the Geats.

Weders, Weder-Geats (13, 86, 122), Geats.

Weland (26), the Völund of the Edda, the famous smith of Teutonic legend, was the maker of Beowulf's coat of mail. See the figured casket in the British Museum; and compare "Wayland Smith's Cave" near the White Horse, in Berkshire.

Weohstan was the father of Beowulf's kinsman and faithful henchman Wiglaf, and the slayer of Eanmund (149).

Wonred, father of "Wulf the Wonreding" (167), and of Eofor.

Wulf (167). *See* Eofor.

Wulfgar, "a lord of the Wendels" (20), is an official of Hrothgar's court, where he is the first to greet Beowulf and his Geats, and introduces them to Hrothgar.

Wythergyld (118) is a warrior of the Heathobards.

THE MEANING OF SOME WORDS NOT COMMONLY USED NOW

(Numbers refer to Pages)

A-banning, the work was (5), orders for the work were given.

Arede (118), possess.

Atheling, prince, noble, noble warrior.

Barm, lap, bosom.

Behalsed (5), embraced by the neck.

Berne, man, warrior, hero.

Bestead (143), served.

Beswealed, scorched, burnt.

Beswinked, sweated.

Birlers, cup-bearers.

Board, shield.

Bode, announce.

Bollen, swollen, angry.

Boot (9), compensation.

Boun (18), made ready.

Braided (147), drew, lifted.

Brim, sea.

Brook, use, enjoy.

Burg, fortified place, stronghold, mount, barrow; protection; protector; family (163).

Byrny, coat of mail.

Devil-dray, nest of devils. Cf. *squirrel's-dray,* common in Berks; used by Cowper.

Dreary, bloody.

Dree, do, accomplish, suffer, enjoy, spend (155).

Ealdor, chief, lord.

Eme, uncle.

Eoten, giant, monster, enemy.

Fathom, embrace.

Feeless, not to be atoned for with money.

Ferry, bring, carry.

Fifel, monster.

Flyting, contending, scolding.

Fold, the earth.

Forheed, disregard.

Forwritten, proscribed.
Frist, space of time, delay.
Gar, spear.
Graithly, readily, well.
Halse, neck.
Hand-shoal, band of warriors.
Hery, praise.
Hild-play, battle.
Holm, ocean, sea.
Holm-throng, eddy of the sea.
Holt, wood.
Hote, call.
Howe, mound, burial-mound.
Hythe, ferry, haven.
Kemp, champion, fighter.
Lithe, slope.
Loom, heirloom.
Low (133), flame.
Lyke, body.
Moody, brave, proud.
Nicors, sea-monsters.
Nithing (12), spite, malice.
O'erthinking, overweening, arrogance.
Rail, railings, coat, armour.

Rimed, counted, reckoned.
Sea-lode, sea-voyage.
Sin, malice, hatred, hostility.
Skinked, poured out.
Slot, track.
Staple, threshold.
Stone-bow, arch of stone.
Sty, stride, ascend, descend.
Sweal, burn.
Through-witting, understanding.
Undern, from 9 o'clock till 12 o'clock; "at undren and at middai," O.E. Miscellany.
Warths, shores, still in use at Wick St. Lawrence, in Somerset.
Wick, dwelling.
Wick-stead, dwelling-place.
Wise, direct, show.
Wit-lust, curiosity.
Worth, shall be.
Wreak, utter.
Wyte, blame, charge with.
Yare, ready.
Yode, went.

Printed by BALLANTYNE, HANSON & Co.
Edinburgh & London